SHADOWS IN THE WIND BOOK TWO

COGITATIO

McKINLEY ASPEN

Cogitatio
Shadows in the Wind: Book Two

Original Cover Art Design: Zachary Fors

This is a work of fiction. Any characters, businesses, places, events, and incidents are either the products of the author's imagination or used in a fictitious manner. Any resemblance to actual persons, living or dead, or actual events is purely coincidental.

Printed in the United States of America

Hardcover ISBN: 978-1-960876-23-2
Paperback ISBN: 978-1-960876-24-9
Ebook ISBN: 978-1-960876-25-6

Library of Congress Control Number: 2023943383

Muse Literary
3319 N. Cicero Avenue
Chicago IL 60641-9998

*"Did you know, my children, that
Cogitatio (pronounced co-gee-tah-tee-o)
is the Latin word for reflection?*

*Sunshine peaking over the mountaintop
reflects into lakes where water mirrors those
sunshine rays as dancing sparkling lights.*

*Is there, therefore, a possibility that
everything is a reflection?*

Perhaps . . ."

~Raphael

DEDICATION

This book is dedicated to
Aunt Margaret

You gave me a book for every occasion,
and even took the time to inscribe
each book with a thoughtful note.

You taught me to love books of all kinds.

I am forever grateful.

PROLOGUE

Fluorescent lighting tends to morph ordinary objects into obscurity. It manipulates colors, distorting light, and shadow.

Lying on my bunk, arms stretched above my head, no covers and wearing shorts and a T-shirt, I still couldn't keep the heat from burning my limbs, sweat trickling over my body as if seeping through to my heart.

The room was lit only by glaring bulbs in the center of the crack-ridden ceiling. If I squinted, the light shifted into dizzying rays that stretched across the ceiling, filling in the cracks and opening up my imagination.

The heat was stifling, way warmer than I'd come to expect in Alaska. I strained to see in this dark room, which was filled with a sound like jet engines.

The sound actually came from industrial fans—they were everywhere. The purpose was twofold: keep the room cool with air movement and mask all other sound—like white noise. I shivered; the fear of being held captive while someone else controlled my every move was eating away at me, despite the warmth of the day.

Women, about forty-five of them, lay on bunk beds around me. My brain was foggy as I jumped off the top bunk into a long body stretch, making my spine crack with each twist. I scanned the room. Other scared, angry, hopeless women, all asleep. These were the people who had become my friends over the months I had been here—people who, I'd learned, no more deserved to be here than I did. Everyone was wearing standard issue gray shorts and white T-shirts.

I was in jail.

In Alaska.

CHAPTER ONE

Shaking my head, I thought, *This must be a dream. Come on, walk out of it, Kathryn. Just walk out.*

But I couldn't. Not this time. This was no dream. I was trapped within the walls of the prison.

Inside this one giant room were sections separated by half-walls. The sleeping area had fifty bunk beds, a bathroom with eight sinks, eight toilets and six showers, and the living room with tables, chairs, a flat-screen television on the wall, an ice cooler, and a hot water spigot. I had never thought of prison like this. Thanks to movies and TV, I had always imagined a six-by-eight cell with one bed, one toilet and sink, and bars.

Although it was grim, the layout and the presence of fifty women reminded me of a freshman college dorm. While drab in color and dispiritingly institutional, it was more frustrating and stressful than oppressive.

This is how each of my days had started for the last ten months. Each morning at 3:45 a.m., I went through this process as if my body had to reconnect to my soul. As I woke and became more aware, I remembered the mission: deep undercover work.

For a moment all I could think about was the entrance to Hope & Global Support (HGS) headquarters. Above the doorway etched in marble, a nod to the early association with the CIA and the ongoing belief in our work, it said, *"The truth shall set you free." John 8:32.*

It had all started back in Manhattan when Raphael asked to meet with me privately. During that meeting, he handed me a set of apartment keys along with an address in Onarde, Alaska.

"This mission will be challenging, Kathryn," he said quietly from behind his old oak desk, sipping on a cup of tea. "And you'll mostly be going it alone."

"But what about the team? I'm the team leader now, shouldn't I be with the team?" I questioned.

"I can tell you that your team will be behind the scenes, supporting you every step of the way." His voice was so low he was nearly whispering, which made me wonder if we were being watched or taped or . . .

"Why are you whispering, Raphael?"

"I want to ensure nobody is listening," he said, staring out the window at a group of blackbirds that had gathered on a nearby branch.

Raphael always seemed to have a conspiracy theory in mind and often said things like this while gazing off into the distance.

"Supporting me to do what?" I continued to dig.

"We continue our task of taking out the crime syndicate, Kate. They're running guns, trafficking drugs, all kinds of devastating crimes. You will be instrumental in identifying all the tentacles of syndicate operations from your position in the upcoming mission," Raphael replied. "For now, head to Alaska and get settled. You will be given housing. Blend in, talk to people—get to know the neighbors. They may very well be our way in. And remember—you are strictly undercover. Don't let anyone know who you really are."

"This all sounds pretty vague."

"Don't worry. The specifics of the mission will be made clear to you. We will be in touch."

"It will be hard to be away from Scott . . ."

"Kate, you know that Scott cannot be a part of this, but I promise, you won't be gone long, probably a year at the most." Raphael reclined in his chair, slowly adding a sugar cube to his tea and stirring it quietly.

"A year?" I had no idea it was going to be a long-term assignment. I was not prepared to hear that.

"What do I have that nobody else on our team can offer?" I asked.

"You are you, and this is all about you right now. Your instinct, your spirit, you are the only candidate for this mission," he said as if there was no other obvious answer.

"I'll try Raphael, but I don't exactly know what I'm looking for." I shrugged.

"They will find you, Kathryn, then you just have to unearth whatever is really going on in Alaska," Raphael said, handing me my documentation. "Good luck."

He stood, shook my hand, and escorted me out the door.

Raphael had provided me with the address of where I would be living, and everything had been prearranged. Scott, my husband, had to stay behind, as this was a mission for just me.

"Kathryn, I need you to do this alone. You are the only one on this team who is strong enough," Raphael had told me. "But no matter where you are, keep the eye with you, pinned somewhere safe. It will always ensure your protection and the protection of those around you."

Raphael was referring to the all-seeing eye, the lapel pin we were each given on the day we started at HGS. The pin was a circle, and at first glance appeared to depict mountains and clouds; however, if you stared at it longer, it shifted into the image of an eyeball. There was a line with fletching at the top (similar to the feathers on the end of an arrow): the staff of protection, according to Raphael. It was the insignia of HGS.

The moment I received the pin, I knew HGS was bigger than just some spy organization.

We were sitting in the conference room, and he passed these small pins around – one for each of us. Each pin was unique, and when you touched it, it gave off a kind of vibration in your hands.

In my palm, the pin distracted me, feeling almost magical, radiant with an energy I couldn't place. I remembered from a history of religion course in college something called "the staff of Raphael," among other things. It was the first time I considered that Raphael might be more than what he appeared to be.

My flight was uneventful, although I did enjoy the beautiful view of snow-topped mountains as we crossed up into Alaska. The first day, its beauty floored me. A verdant tangle of pine, fir, and spruce trees stretched across the land and up mountains wreathed in mist. The air was crisp and unlike any other; it was as if I was feeling, tasting, and experiencing oxygen for the first time. Each breath filled me with a sense of hope, a sense of adventure, and a sense of the unknown.

My condo was close to the Gulf of Alaska. This was wonderful for me, as I loved living near big bodies of water. When I pulled up, I immediately noticed the dark grey cedar exterior, and how well kept the complex was with several flower beds and trees surrounding it.

My unit was on the second floor (the top floor). The place was surprisingly light and bright. I had expected less, as I had been told it was rugged in parts of Alaska, so this was a pleasant surprise. It was painted neutral beige, with trim reminiscent of 1970s wood trim that I remembered seeing in my friends' houses. Still, it was nice, clean, and quiet.

Several boxes of basic necessities had been shipped prior to my arrival and were neatly stacked adjacent to the entryway. I immediately got to work, lugging box after box to the proper room for unpacking, when I realized I had left my two pieces of luggage in the car. As I was wrestling with getting the two bags up to the second floor, I met my downstairs neighbor, Tom.

At six feet three with blonde hair, slightly overweight, and a face full of wrinkles, he could have easily been mistaken for being older than he was.

As we shook hands, I felt a zap of electrical current. What he said next stopped me in my tracks.

"I know we literally just met, but I have to say that I feel like I could trust you with my life," Tom said. He had a firm handshake, yet his hands were noticeably soft, as if he had never worked a day in his life. He was rather effeminate in nature.

Had I misheard?

"Wait, what?" I spoke.

"Just that. I feel like I could trust you with my life."

"I, uh, have to go," I said. And I walked away quickly, feeling my face flush and my blood race through my veins. I had no word for what I was feeling after that bizarre interaction with Tom, but I knew I had to get away from it.

"Wait, wait!" Tom yelled, clamoring after me up the stairs, "let me help you."

"I've got it!" My body was trying to get as far in front of him as possible, while my brain was trying to remember where the frying pan was so I could unpack it and use it as a weapon.

"Listen, just take a minute please. When we shook hands, I felt something, like a zap when you walk on the carpet in the wintertime. You can't tell me you didn't feel it?" He ran his fingers through blonde hair in a way that reminded me of the greasers from the old 1950s movies.

I was worried. I *had* felt that.

"I felt it," I stammered. "Must have been winter shock, a little static." It happens all the time in cold and dry climates. "Thanks for the help," I nodded as I politely shut the door in his face.

CHAPTER TWO

The next morning I was returning from my walk when I saw Tom from a distance. I didn't want to interact with him again, but I had to pass him to get up the stairs, so I did my best to be gracious but kept moving.

"Good morning," Tom grinned. "How was your first night in Alaska?"

"It was fine, thank you." I didn't make eye contact, I just kept moving up the stairs; however, Tom was quick to follow.

"So what brings you to Alaska?"

"My job."

"Oh, what do you do?" He leaned in with a hair toss.

"Marketing," I said dismissively, jostling my key in the lock, eager to hear that satisfying, reassuring click that signaled an open door. BE ON ALERT my body was telling me.

"We've lived here a few years. My wife and I have been married a while, and we have twin girls."

"Oh, that's nice." I raised my hands in the air stretching, only half paying attention. I was trying to figure out why this man was home at 10:30 a.m. on a Tuesday.

"I have a landscaping business, but in the winter, I do other odd jobs like housekeeping and maintenance, so I pretty much make my own schedule."

"Okay, well, have a nice—"

"I've got to get going, but I will see you around," he interrupted. He just upped and left. As suddenly as he arrived, he was gone. The abruptness of it reminded me of a child switching a toy from off to on – it was like someone had pressed a control button and switched him from "stay" to "leave."

The next day and the day after that followed the same pattern. Me going about my day, taking a morning or afternoon walk, and Tom showing up randomly. He was trying hard to buddy up to me, but I wasn't having it. That simple question, "Why are you here in Alaska?" should have been my initial clue. The very first thing anyone understands once they actually get to Alaska is that there is a lot of space, not many people. And nobody asks why you are there, how you got there, or anything like that. It is frowned upon. Instead, they just welcome you and do not pry into the "why." I found their discretion refreshing. An unspoken acceptance without question. In Alaska, people mind their own business.

Other things were off too. Tom's seasonal landscaping business somehow afforded him the ability to take off during the lean months and provide for his family year-round. I suppose it was possible, but I had known landscapers; most of them barely got by. And by the look of the expensive SUV parked outside, the designer clothes fitting him to perfection, the Rolex on his wrist—Is that real, or is it a perfect knockoff? —he was doing a lot more than just "getting by."

During every one of our stilted interactions in the coming days, he repeated his question about why I was in Alaska, what was my job exactly, who did I work for.

"Job changes," was all I said.

To my relief, Tom dropped the subject, and I relaxed.

The next day, there was a knock at the door, and there was Tom with two drinks in hand.

"Hot tea?" he asked, smiling as he walked in.

While I found some of his mannerisms off-putting, I was also starting to warm to him. I admitted to myself that I was probably just lonely and in need of a friend.

Since I was on a solo assignment, that meant I didn't have the opportunity to speak to Scott, or anyone else from the team, so it was a nice distraction that he was really making an effort to connect with me.

Perhaps he was just being neighborly, just wanted me to feel welcomed? I wasn't sure what to think. It seemed like the more he spoke, the more he made it sound like we had several things in common. He was clearly a master distractor, one of those people who always has you looking one way while he's manipulating something else behind your back.

"So, have you been married long?" I asked, shuffling books out of boxes and continuing to get settled.

"About fifteen years, but we have been together for twenty," he replied as he plopped into one of the living room chairs.

"What does that mean 'been together'?" I asked, twisting around towards him.

"Oh, we met and dated a bit and then got serious about five years into it. We had the twins a few months after we were married, and well, here we are."

I didn't know how to respond.

"Are you okay?" he asked. "You are so quiet. Did I say something wrong?"

"No, it's just . . . No, nothing."

"Hey, you gotta come over for dinner, and Jessica would love to meet you. How about tonight?"

The unexpected invitation left me floundering for an excuse.

"Well . . .I don't know, I'm pretty busy," I said. On a mission, you had to be wary of everyone. I still didn't like the sudden interest he had taken in me, and I knew accepting a dinner invitation would just give him more opportunity to pry.

It was times like this when I missed having Scott, Michael, Greg, all of them around. I missed everyone most days, but Michael and I had a friendship that was open and honest, fully transparent without judgement, and that was rare.

I think Scott respected our friendship sometimes because he just didn't understand it. We didn't either. It's like we were tied at the hip. These moments made me miss looking across the room to get some additional insight and seeing him make a goofy face or roll his eyes or something.

I really wish I knew what this assignment was all about and that I could call someone from our team—it was hard being incommunicado. It made life lonely.

"My wife and daughters are going to like you. Hey, are you married?"

The correct answer was yes, but I couldn't say that because I was on assignment undercover.

"I'm in a relationship. As for dinner, let's see how it goes. Can we play it by ear?"

Of course, I went to dinner. There was something so persuasive about Tom—that shy smile, those droopy glassed-over eyes, which I thought were sweet—but yet another red flag I never saw coming.

"Thanks for coming to dinner! It's nice to meet you."

Jessica. A stocky woman with wrinkled skin who looked like she had seen one too many days in the sun. This was coupled with way too many hair-coloring and Botox sessions. Was she trying too hard, or just being friendly? Did that smile reach her eyes? Was her voice a bit too clipped to be natural? Was she just shy maybe?

What I wouldn't give for Ashley's clairsentient skill right now.

"Likewise." I sat down and tried to look more comfortable than I was feeling.

Dinner turned out to be fun, despite all my misgivings. Tom was engaging company and kept me laughing with a string of anecdotes about life in the lawn business and various oddball experiences.

The little girls, Nance and Nell, were undeniably tomboys whose femininity occasionally flashed on the surface. With bright sparkling green eyes and red hair that seemed to be frizz in all directions, they were kind and inquisitive, just as most children are.

"Do you like Alaska?" Nell asked.

"What is that pin you are wearing?" Nance jumped in before I could answer. At first, I thought she meant my HGS pin, which was "hidden" under my collar as I normally wore it. However, she was pointing to my ornamental hairpin. I crouched into a catcher's stance to look them each in the eye.

"Well, Nancy, I like Alaska. I don't know much about it quite yet but I'm learning." Then, turning my focus to the other, "and Nell, as for this pin, I was given it by a friend for good luck." I touched it and smiled.

Actually, it was from my father. It had belonged to my grandmother. My own mother never had long hair, so it sat in a drawer for a long time, unused, until Dad found a suitable owner for it.

"Ah kids, always so inquisitive," Tom chuckled.

Jessica laughed too. But when I met her eye, I caught a glimmer of a look. A fleeting glance that was as cold as ice. Then she smiled a sunny smile, and the ice thawed.

Looking back at the twins, I removed the pin from my hair and held it in my outstretched palm. "The good luck it provides is real. So take care of it."

"We can keep it?" asked a wide-eyed Nancy. Her sister took it from my hand and held it to the light like a jeweler looking at a ruby with his loupe.

"Sure you can. My gift to you. Just share."

I looked back at Jessica, half-expecting another glare, but her attention was on Tom.

The kids went to bed, and the rest of the evening was uneventful. Had I imagined Jessica's hostility? Possible. But unlikely.

Within several weeks, these people had squeezed themselves into my life. My heart has always been ten times larger than it should be. I have always been quick to trust people, perhaps more so than they deserved. Still feeling out of sorts from not being with Scott and the team every day, and unsure of my mission, I clung to my new friends and the comfort they offered, and they seemed to relish the time we spent together as much as I did. If I wasn't sharing a coffee with Jessica, I was helping Tom with his business or answering a question the girls had about school projects. Plus, it wasn't a one-way street—Tom and Jessica helped me so much with settling in during those early days in Alaska, and she turned out to be an absolute star when it came to fixing things around the condo.

By the end of the month, I had a set of sturdy shelves in my sitting room and bedroom, my leaky faucet was leaky no more, and I was able to replace the mishmash of inherited plates and bowls with a nice kitchen set that Tom and Jessica just had lying around. If I sometimes perceived the ice in Jessica's gaze when we were all together, I noted that she was always friendly and fun to be around when it was just the two of us. Was she jealous? Did she think I was making a move on her husband? If we were to be the real friends, as I felt we were becoming, we needed to have no secrets between us. Well, none other than those essential to the mission—like the fact that I had superpowers, was married to a man with superpowers, and worked with colleagues who possessed superpowers . . .you know, the small details. Other than that, I wanted my friendship with Tom and Jessica to be as open and straightforward as possible, and so I resolved to have a woman-to-woman chat with Jessica and make sure there were no bad feelings between us.

However, I never got the chance to have that chat.

Without warning, police officers came to my door.

CHAPTER THREE

"We have a warrant for your arrest."

There were two of them, one male, one female. And they meant business.

"Me?"

"You."

"What did I do?"

"We can discuss that at the station."

My brain was on fire. What should I do? I'd seen people on television in this very scenario, but I couldn't remember if they let the police into their homes or not. What about rights—does anybody actually read you your rights?

"Can I grab my purse? My phone?"

"Grab them, and let's go."

"Why are you following me?" I asked as I walked to the other room to grab my purse.

"I can't let you out of my sight, you are in my custody now," the female officer replied.

What was happening? I was not even safe in my own home.

This was not like I had seen on television. No reading of the rights, nothing like that. Just here we go, and bam! I was in the back of a car in handcuffs, and it looked like the whole neighborhood had turned out to watch.

"What are my charges?" I demanded. But I received nothing but stony silence.

"Where's Sarge?" one officer yelled.

"He's grabbing evidence, he'll be right out."

Evidence? I mean, what in the world? I haven't done anything!

I heard the thumps of several items they took from my condo and threw into the trunk, and then the lid slammed down. One of the officers climbed into the passenger seat, looking back at me, his face a mask of contempt. His colleague climbed in behind the steering wheel, not even looking at me as she exchanged a judgmental glance with him, shifted the car into gear, and started to drive away.

I lowered my eyes, not wanting to meet anyone's accusing gaze, not wanting to see Tom and Jessica witnessing my humiliation. At the last moment, as I was driven away in the police car, I raised my eyes and looked back at the people I had considered friends.

My eyes locked with Tom's for a second, but instead of the support I had hoped for, or the judgment I had feared, all I saw in him was . . . nothing. Tom was expressionless. He dropped his gaze to the ground, turned, and disappeared into the condo below mine.

Then I locked eyes with Jessica, and my blood froze. Her face was a mask of spite. Spite and triumph and glaring red eyes. Red? At that very moment, the police car picked up speed and the sirens kicked in, their wail echoing the chaos of my thoughts, and I realized how stupid I had been.

Had my new friends somehow betrayed me? If so, why? And how?

I didn't have to wait long to find out why I had been betrayed. I had been arrested on charges of trafficking cocaine. Me! It was unfathomable. I am about as anti-drug as one can get. I enjoy being worn out at the end of each day and relaxing with a ginger ale and a cherry. I detested the drug scene even more since I learned how it led to the death of Ashley's brother. I hardly drink alcohol, let alone take any meds, but that didn't alter the fact that the cops found cocaine with a street value of around $3 million in my condo, along with loads of cash. To my knowledge, all I had in the condo was milk, toast, and cans of soup—while I was secretly sitting on millions of dollars and living like a pauper. This didn't add up.

"That's a heck of a lot of coke to use in a setup!" I exclaimed when I learned this little gem of information. The police officers stopped—the same officers who had driven me to the holding facility. The bigger one, who had to weigh at least three hundred pounds, glared at me with contempt. The other, who was slender and short with a pimply nose, exuded hatred. I seemed to be eliciting a lot of hatred today.

"That's a heck of a lot of coke to be dealing with kids," the officer sneered. "We found it in your condo."

"I don't understand all of this. Isn't there something I can do?" I asked. "Aren't we supposed to be innocent until proven guilty?"

"You will be held until you can get bailed out—that is, if the judge even grants bail—and then you can go about figuring out how to prove that you are not guilty," the skinny one said, scratching her ear like a dog with fleas.

The heavier one chimed in. "No way you're getting bail though. Not for this amount of coke. It's people like you that we need off of our streets and out of our society."

This was a game to them. A game, or a joke, or something. They didn't care about me, not one stitch. Was anybody going to actually help me? What was going on?

"We have eyewitness accounts that you've been using kids as young as ten to do your running for you. You're in serious trouble, lady, so I suggest you keep your drug-dealing mouth shut, or I may have to shut it for you."

"Kids? I'd never . . ."

"Two girls, living in the condo below yours? Remember them? Age ten, so their mom tells us. She can't believe you'd use her kids in your sick trade . . ."

"Jessica told you what?"

"I told you to SHUT IT!" The cop was right in my face now. I could smell the coffee on her breath, a hint of stale garlic from last night's meal, and the underlying halitosis. It was all I could do not to recoil, but my disgust must have been apparent because she smiled coldly.

"Whatever you're thinking, it's no way as bad as what I think of you, lady. Your neighbors called it in. Something about how you pretended to be their friend . . ."

How ironic. That's what I'd thought about them.

"Claimed to the officer that they had no choice but to protect their kids from you, and all the kids in the neighborhood."

So, Jessica and Tom had betrayed me. I could see I wasn't going to convince this cop of that, though. Innocent until proven guilty? What a joke. What a messed-up system. This experience had already begun to challenge my patriotism and my belief in the justice system itself. What about due process? Had any of these guys even read the Constitution?

In the eyes of the officer, I was already tried and convicted. My best option—for now, it seemed—was to do as I was told. Surely, this was part of Raphael's plans. I wondered if he had created this ruse on purpose. I was getting used to Raphael telling me and the team little to no detail about the missions, but having me arrested on drug charges? This was something else.

Raphael was strategic and shrewd in everything he did. Could it be that he was testing me—ensuring that by surprising me with this arrest, I would have to rely on my instincts and quick thinking rather than foreplaning? Or maybe it was so that I could blend in with the other inmates—for now, I truly was one too. I was one of them.

As Raphael always reminded me, "So long as you do what feels right with what you see, things will often work out better than human averages dictate."

After that, I was locked in a holding cell for nine hours. No food or drink, just a peculiar smell of recycled air—fresh and stagnant at the same time. There was a bank of "free" phones on one wall—free if the call was to a landline in the United States. By this time, I had nothing with me— my purse, wallet, and phone had been confiscated and placed in a secure location until the cops figured out what to do with me.

With difficulty, tucking the receiver under my chin while I dialed, I called Scott's office.

It never dawned on me that the call would be recorded, so when I heard him say hello and a voice responded, "Will you accept a call from federal holding in Seward, Alaska?" I was shocked and embarrassed and felt like screaming and crying all at once.

I heard him say, "I will accept" and the call was connected.

"Scott?" It was the only word I got out before he started talking.

"Arrested?" his voice squeaked into the other end of the phone. Uh-oh, a surprise reaction didn't seem quite right. If the arrest had been somehow orchestrated by Raphael, he would have given Scott the heads-up. My mind began to reel. What if this wasn't Raphael's doing?

"Arrested. I am so glad you answered because they said you can only dial landlines, so I wasn't even sure what to do."

"I was actually just packing up for the day." He trailed off. "What did you do?"

"Nothing, nothing! What d'you take me for?"

"Okay, okay, I meant to say, what have they accused you of?"

"You wouldn't believe me if I told you."

"Try me."

"Drugs." My voice broke, and I cleared my throat before I could continue. "I've been accused of selling drugs . . . dealing cocaine. They found $3 million worth in my condo, and they say I've been recruiting kids to . . ."

Speaking the words out loud, I realized the enormity of the accusations and broke down completely.

"Okay, listen—LISTEN! We don't have much time," Scott's voice was garbled like he was juggling the phone and trying to write at the same time.

I controlled myself with an effort, sniffling at him to go on.

"Do you want me to step into this?"

"No, but please call Raphael and tell him, okay?"

"Okay. I don't like this. I feel helpless, but I will call Raphael. I love you."

"I love you t—" My phone call timed out and disconnected.

Back on the hard bench in the holding cell, I was cold and didn't have a jacket with me. The room was full of women, but barely a word was spoken. Everyone was just sitting, staring into space, their faces mirroring the confusion I felt. Something about the grim silence was eerie.

A surly guard patrolling the room came and talked to us. We were separated from the men in a holding cell on the other side of a dividing wall. We could not just go to the bathroom; we had to ask an officer, who would allow us to go one at a time.

It had been nearly ten hours. Ten hours of just sitting in this miserable room. Ten hours and the door unlocked, and we were moved. An officer—luckily not the judgmental one who had charged me—came and took us to fingerprint. Then, we all had our photographs taken.

"Don't smile," she commanded just before the camera flashed. As if any of us felt like smiling. Then we were all given clothes—navy sweatpants and sweatshirts with socks and shoes that reminded me of Crocs—and taken to a holding dormitory. We were given blankets, a cup, a bar of soap, a toothbrush and toothpaste, and "boats"—a plastic cot that we had to place on the floor. Yes, the holding officers had us sleeping on the floor because there had been so many people arrested that day. If my mind hadn't been so clouded by confusion, sadness at my so-called friends' betrayal, and—yes, I admit it—icy cold fear, I might have wondered why that was.

That night was one of the longest nights of my life. I didn't get any sleep at all, I didn't feel safe. There were girls screaming, seemingly detoxing, and others chattering endlessly. Even after the lights were turned out, not an ounce of privacy was to be found, so I put my head under my blanket and created my own "tent" and tried to retreat into a space of silence.

On my second day, I was called into a room with forty other women and a video monitor showing a judge. A court-appointed defense lawyer was present (we were told that is customary), but he seemed half-asleep, almost semi-coherent (was he drunk?), and all-around incompetent.

This meeting was referred to as "first appearance" and they called each of us in the room up to the monitor and basically told us what we were accused of. In front of everybody, no privacy. It made me wonder if the whole "innocent until proven guilty" thing was real or not, because the system just seemed to be eager to direct blame and pass judgement on each and every woman who stepped up.

No matter the embarrassment of having your private details listed out in front of perfect strangers, what was even stranger was that nobody disputed anything. Everyone just replied the same "yes, your honor" and left the room. It was as if there was really no other option. So, I followed suit and did the same.

Scott had told me not to talk to anybody if I could help it, and certainly not to discuss my charges with anyone, but that wasn't possible after the forty people heard my charge that morning. Word spread like wildfire: apparently, I was a badass, a mastermind, a kingpin in the drug world.

I tried to keep to myself. Sitting most of the day on my bunk. There wasn't anything to do (unless I went to the open area and watched TV), nothing to read (unless I asked someone to borrow a magazine or book) so I just sat there thinking, staring, thinking.

The room had a bank of what they called "free phones," which meant if you stood in line and were able to get a turn, you would have ten minutes to call someone for free. The phone call timed out after ten minutes, so I was preparing my thoughts when a younger blonde girl glanced at me and pointed to her phone. She was finishing up and readying to give me her spot, and I quickly moved over to take it.

I dialed the numbers with my freezing cold fingers. Everything here was cold, and I found myself in a constant state of shivering.

I heard the operator say, "Will you accept a call from the detention center?" followed by Scott saying, "Yes" and then "Hello?"

"Hi."

"Oh, I am so glad to hear your voice." Scott's voice was gentle and calming. "I've been trying to 'find you' but cannot pinpoint exactly where you are. Are you okay? What's going on?"

"I don't know where to start, but yes, I guess I'm okay. It's freezing here and I'm not sure what is happening, it's like the same day every single day over and over again. No guidance or any idea of anything at this point."

"I spoke to Raphael, and just so you know, he was concerned, but you should know he is very aware of the situation."

My entire body relaxed. Somehow, Raphael was involved in this situation, and I would be okay.

"Thank you for telling me that." I knew I couldn't say much more. The calls were short, and recorded, and I had no idea what was to come next.

"I am going to try and do a video call with you in a few days if we can figure out how to set it up, and I'm asking some people I know about how things are handled," Scott added, sounding like the professional legal expert.

"Thanks. I'm trying, it's all I can do. I don't understand any of this."

"I know, I know—just keep to yourself and we will be together soon."

CLICK.

Time was up. I sat for a moment trying to take in all of what I heard, and what he hadn't disclosed—reading between the lines.

RAPHAEL IS AWARE OF THE SITUATION.

Fast forward to day five, when I was woken up at midnight and told I would be transferred to a more permanent location three hours away.

At three a.m., I was taken in a van with thirty other women, none of whom resembled hardened criminals. We all just looked like sad and confused women who had been torn unexpectedly from our daily lives and flung into a hostile and unfamiliar world. From the looks on the faces around me, it was one that none of us deserved to be a part of.

At Scott's direction I hadn't spoken to anyone while I was there. I just kept to myself and stayed in my boat. I immediately wondered how I would be able to let Scott know where I was. Would he be able to find out I had been moved? This seemed very 'covert' for the justice system – 3:00 a.m. and all.

But now, as I sat on this bus wondering what the future offered me, I noticed many things. The first thing that struck me was that we were all on a bus. Although everyone was handcuffed, there were no bars on the bus, it was just a bus, and we were all sitting like elementary students on a field trip. Many of the women just stared out the window, watching the countryside roll by, and I was watching them watch the scenery.

I glanced up a few rows to notice a big head of billowing curly red hair—naturally curly and frizzy and piled up in a knot on top of the head like the girls with big hair that was so popular in the '80s.

Like a lightning bolt, the recognition penetrated my numb brain, and a fresh glimmer of hope flickered in me.

"Hey," I whispered.

"Yeah?" my neighbor responded in a grunt.

"Poke that woman next to you and get her to look at me," I asked.

"The one with the tattoo on her neck?"

"No, the one with the frizzy curly red hair near the window."

"Why, you like her or something?" The woman flashed an impish grin.

"No, just do it."

Two pokes later, the woman in question reluctantly lifted her head. Her face was blotchy, showcasing days of shock and tears. She looked at the woman who had poked her, but before she had a chance to say anything, she noticed me sitting on the other side.

Mouth open, she just stared at me. The flicker of hope ignited. I had been right. She was who I thought she was.

Ashley Harrington. My Ashley. My HGS team member.

I nodded. Ashley nodded back, and we both took deep breaths. Was this something significant I'd been waiting for? Was this what Raphael had alluded to? Whatever it was, things had suddenly gotten a whole lot better for both of us.

The van pulled into a gravel driveway and stopped. The back doors were thrown open and a tall, thin woman in blue pants, a blue shirt, and work boots stood silhouetted by the rising sun. Beyond her, I could make out a paved courtyard surrounded by four brick buildings, each single story in height with square windows set at regular intervals. Although it said CORRECTIONAL CENTER on the front, it reminded me of an old folk's home, with barbed wire.

So, here we were. No *Law and Order*-esque trial for the real people, just a judge on a monitor and then straight off to prison. Guilty until proven otherwise. How could this be, in a free country? Innocence, freedom, rights. My faith in the system was shattered.

"Everybody out of the van. Walk in a line over this way, please," the woman commanded. "My name is Ms. Spearfish. I am in charge of bringing you in and getting you organized. Follow me inside." I sensed her bristly, rough-around-the-edges exterior was mostly just for show. I hoped I was right.

Ms. Spearfish led us into a library where chairs had been set up conference-style with a front desk. A middle-aged woman with a slender figure and dark hair that was just starting to show a hint of gray; she didn't seem arrogant and domineering like the cops in the holding facility.

The library captivated me immediately. Not only were there rows and rows of books (yes, a true library), but the color was such an unusual mint-seafoam green. As if someone had mixed all the leftover paint colors and this is what they had come up with.

The floor was covered by indoor-outdoor carpet, muffling sound as it was walked on. The hallway that had led us here had been dead quiet, and the room was eerily silent.

"Welcome," said Ms. Spearfish. "This is the library—you will get to come back here once a week, sometimes more. In the meantime, though, let's get started. Everybody will be given soap and towels to take a shower. Private showers are right across the hallway. Then, we will give you sets of clean clothes. Once you are showered and changed, come back in here and sit down."

Private showers? I wondered about this because I was quite sure we wouldn't have private anything. Just as the thought passed my mind, a younger looking slender blonde woman came in dressed in khaki pants and gym shoes. She smiled as she handed out bags filled with towels, soap, shampoo, and clothes. She then took two of us at a time to shower and change.

Already this was different from where I had been held. Private showers, curtains, someone actually gave me shampoo and a towel to use, and I felt respected; not 100 percent but still respected all the same.

"Okay," Ms. Spearfish continued, "Before we get started, let me be crystal clear. This is the beginning of a new life for each of you. We don't care what happened in the past, where you came from, or even what you may or may not have done. This is your chance to choose a different direction."

Everyone just sat there, dumbfounded. It was as if nobody really knew what to do, what to say, or how to react. I wondered why these people were here. I wondered why I was here.

Ms. Spearfish continued, "If you are wondering how you might do that, well, you might consider joining our choir or softball team or even working in the school teaching others. There are arts and crafts classes, church, and other activities you can explore. You will also be given jobs, and you might find that you learn a skill you never had before, so try to remain open-minded and curious."

This did not sound like what I thought prison was going to be.

"This is Kim," she said, gesturing to a woman standing next to her, "and she will be assigning each of you to dorms and beds. Then we will take you to your dorm to get settled."

Kim, a tall, slender blonde around thirty years old, stood up and began to read off last names along with dorm numbers and bed numbers.

My spirits lifted when I heard "Harrington, Dorm 1 Bed 6; Bek Dorm 1 Bed 22."

Ashley and I were in the same dorm. We were close enough to keep an eye on each other, but far enough away to make communication somewhat tricky. However, importantly, we'd ended up in the same van and the same room. Coincidence? Who knew? But what a relief it was. It was, however, tempered by a new concern: I was supposed to be operating under an alias, but somehow, they knew my real name. Was my cover blown?

As we walked across the campus to our dorm, we noticed the freshly planted flowers and the expansive lawns. There was a porch on the back of our dorm, and we had windows that overlooked the meadow, so we got to see the sunset every afternoon with the western windows.

What is this place, really? I found it bizarre that a prison would be like this. Just one more thing that made me think that maybe all of us here weren't that awful after all, and maybe the system truly had just failed, and we were going to be making the best of it.

I put my things away in my assigned closet locker, thinking of the colorful kitchen units that my so-called friend Jessica had made for me. No, I had to put these negative thoughts out of my head. No wallowing in self-pity. After all, now I was reunited with Ashley—a friend I knew I could trust.

I lay down on my bed. All I could do at this point was face the facts. I didn't want the notoriety, the publicity, the slander. I didn't want to be a troublemaker. I just wanted to move through whatever this madness was with grace and ease— 'failles' as Raphael called us, 'shadows' moving through the world; but, when trouble found me, I was determined I would be ready, as I knew it eventually would.

CHAPTER FOUR

"Good work! Better than I could have ever expected." The woman she knew as Ms. Raven handed Jessica a blank envelope.

"Thanks." Jessica took the envelope, opened the edge with her thumb, and peeked inside. It was bulging with one-hundred-dollar bills.

"That's just the beginning, Jessica. You keep doing good work like this on my special projects, and there's more of that for you and Tom and your children."

"Thank you. We can sure use this."

Ms. Raven merely smiled coldly, and Jessica giggled nervously in return. She had a deep admiration – intercut with an intense fear – for this elegant woman.

"What's next? What else can I do to be of assistance?" she asked, curiosity burning her up inside. What had caused Ms. Raven's interest in her new neighbor? Why had the woman been so set on incarcerating Kathryn? It didn't matter; it was a great deal of money for only a little bit of work. And Tom? Well, Tom was mad, but he would get over it.

Tom was not the most stand-uppish guy in the world. *After all, ever since I caught him cheating on me and held his feet to the fire, he's been like a dopey little pet on a leash doing whatever I say and never questioning the choices I make,* Jessica thought.

"Sanchez—come in here."

"Yes, ma'am." Dressed in a navy suit and tie, white broadcloth shirt, and shined shoes, a dark-haired, clean-shaven man entered the room, his eyes scanning the corners to ensure everything was as it should be. Ms. Raven's henchmen might not have been the sharpest pencils in the box, but they were loyal—no one could ever say otherwise.

"Sanchez, take Jessica over to the headquarters building—I am promoting her to senior administrator for the Pacific Northwest. She will be the head administrator for all Paolucci family operations. All administrative tasks and requests will run through her."

"Oh, well—um, thank you, Ms. Raven," Jessica replied meekly, her eyes widening. Had she just received a huge promotion? Would this mean a higher salary, more prestige? The thrill of it was offset by stirrings of unease in the pit of her stomach, not helped by the fact the brooding Sanchez terrified her almost as much as Ms. Raven herself.

"No, Jessica, thank you, and what about your husband, Tom? You both stepped up when the family needed you; that won't be forgotten. Why did he not attend this meeting with you today, as invited?"

"We couldn't get a sitter for the kids," Jessica lied. She was angry with her husband—didn't he get that she was doing this work for the kids, to assure only the best for them?

"Well, you will have to tell him when you get back home."

Jessica didn't share that Tom had actually left town with the children. Headed to his mom's home near Miami, bleating some pathetic excuse about how she never saw them. It was hardly surprising when the stupid woman had decided to stay in hot, miserable, overcrowded Miami rather than join them in their new life in Alaska.

Jessica and her mother-in-law had never been friends. *Hopefully, the conniving old dragon will let my husband fly back home as promised, and not get her claws in and force him to stay. He better be home when I get back.* However, deep down, Jessica was aware of an unsettling truth—she was glad her daughters were far away from Alaska. Far away from this terrifying woman in front of her.

When Jessica realized she had been staring at her feet the whole time these thoughts had been running through her head, she lifted her eyes and smiled as genuinely as she could muster. Ms. Raven was gazing back at her with eyes as black as the darkest night, as empty as the farthest reaches of space. There was no humanity in that gaze, and Jessica shivered.

Ms. Raven smiled, but it did nothing to soften the icy hardness of her face.

"I expect you're looking forward to getting started in your new role. Sanchez?"

Crossing the room to stand in front of Jessica, Sanchez held out a hand, indicating she should precede him through the door.

"After you," he said.

"Good-bye, Jessica," called Ms. Raven, the note of finality in her voice causing a slight whimper to escape from Jessica's lips. With Sanchez's hand against the small of her back, propelling her along just on the right side of forcefully, she had no choice but to go with the man, the cackle of Ms. Raven's laugh and the *click-click* of her Jimmy Choo heels following them down the corridor.

CHAPTER FIVE

Three forty-five in the morning, another Friday, another day waking up in prison. I could see the glimmer of daylight through the upper windows. I got up, made my bed, and headed to the communal bathroom to get ready for the day. We couldn't take showers in the morning. There was some rule (which nobody could explain) that said the showers would be "turned on" at 2:00 p.m. and then turned off at 11:00 p.m. No showers outside of that period. However, there was a big, oversized utility sink at the end of a row of regular sinks. Many of the women would use the big sink to wash their hair and ensure they were fresh and presentable for the day.

Once I was done getting ready, I would sit, read an early morning devotional, and then wake up Ashley. I am not overly religious; however, one of the things they do give everyone to read is a monthly devotional pamphlet. It was something I could do to occupy my thoughts and eliminate the fear and stress I was experiencing moment to moment.

After I finished reading, I would wake up two or three other women and they would get ready, finish, and then wake up a few others, and so it went. This way everyone had their own time in the bathroom to get ready. Somehow, in a room full of fifty women, we had made the morning and evening routines seamless.

Yes, sometimes confrontations happened. But the mornings and evenings were like slivers of normal life where we each had a moment, and nobody wanted to mess that up. In other times, there were disagreements, yelling, screaming, hairpulling, you name it, but nobody dared to mess with the morning or evening routines. It fascinated me that people who were so cranky, angry, catty, and quick to blame were calm and easygoing when they focused on their own shower time.

Every day I was thankful for Ashley. We had to remain reasonably distant initially, but then we started to talk. We figured that way nobody would think we had already known each other – if someone suspected that, it was asking for trouble.

In the months we'd been here—still no lawyers, no trial, no hint that our cases were moving through the justice system, and our questions to prison officials went unanswered—but at least we were together, in the same dormitory. I had become familiar with the other women in the dorm. I guess that's what happens when you spend twenty-four hours a day with people, you get to know everything about them—their stories, their past, their idiosyncrasies.

Cliques of women formed. Many people would just hang out with others whose bed was adjacent. Others might have a job during the day and work with someone and get to know them that way, but oftentimes people who worked together were not in the same dormitory.

I had surrounded myself with a group of women whose beds were near mine: Christina, Wanda, Caprice, and AB. I found out that I was not alone. Like me, they and others had been arrested without evidence or under questionable circumstances. Some had been offered a "deal" and took it, not to admit guilt, but just to be done with everything and not have the drama and expense of a trial. Or sometimes prosecutors held over their heads the prospect of draconian sentences if they were convicted in trial, forcing them to accept a bad plea deal as the lesser of two evils. The system didn't care if they were guilty or innocent.

Scott instructed me not to talk about specifics of the case with others, so I tended to keep my own information private, but many of these women wanted to talk, so I listened. They all agreed it made them feel better to get things off their chests, and the more I heard, the more I questioned the justice system.

While I had been arrested for having millions of dollars' worth of cocaine, Krystal had been arrested for robbing a bank. Just as in my case where the police couldn't prove that I was a drug dealer—much less that I even had the drugs—they also couldn't prove that Krystal was even inside a bank on the day of the supposed robbery.

"What do you mean you were charged with robbing a bank, but you weren't even there?" I asked.

"I was in the bank the day before it happened, and they claim that I was the 'mastermind' of the operation," Krystal replied. "Actually, I am glad to be here because I was on the street and my pimp was running my life, so this got me out of an awful situation – I view it as a good thing. But still, he did it all and set me up, but there's no telling a judge that – they just don't want to listen. And my public defender could care less. I am hopeful that when I get released, I can go somewhere else and start fresh. While I'm here, I'm going to study to get my GED so that's a start."

"Well, I think you're right. Even though it's a bad situation, you might be better off here than on the streets. Maybe this is a blessing in disguise." I tried to be encouraging while not even knowing where to start.

Wanda was around forty, with short hair and bright eyes. "Well, if you think that story is messed up, let me tell you mine," she began. "I was working for a small family as their bookkeeper and the owners were doing a bunch of things that I was unaware of; however, when push came to shove and they were accused of 'inappropriate business handling,' they all pointed to 'the bookkeeper' and here I am." Wanda shook her head. "They even came to my house and dragged me out of bed in the middle of the night . . . so dramatic and certainly not necessary, and absolutely something I will need years of therapy for."

"Oh, Wanda, I'm sad to hear that."

"It just goes to show you that anybody will screw you over and nobody truly has your back. If they can finger someone else to take the spotlight off of themselves, they will do it. Humans are just lame."

"Caprice, what about you?" I asked.

A thickset woman with Polynesian features, gleaming eyes, and jet-black hair stared back at me. "Well, Kate, you haven't told us about you yet," she said.

"Oh, with me there isn't much to tell, so let's focus on you. We really want to help and if it helps you to talk to us, we are here to listen." At this point we had moved our discussion to one of the tables in the open area, along with our snacks and drinks, and we were just waiting for what she had to say.

"Well, um, I was charged with attempted murder—trying to kill my ex-fiancé."

"Oh." I gulped down my feelings as this really caught me off guard.

"Wow, that's something serious. What did you actually do, Caprice?" Krystal leaned closer.

"It wasn't like that."

"Was there a gun involved, or was it poison or . . ." Wanda asked, allowing her question to trail off for effect. "Maybe there is a movie to be made," Wanda added with a smile, trying to lighten the mood.

"No, okay so . . . please don't laugh because I feel terrible about this. Basically, he broke off our engagement because he found someone else."

"Happens," Krystal nodded.

"Yeah, right? So, I went over to his place and stole his cat." She paused. "I figured, break it off with me, I'm taking the cat. Well, I stopped to put gas in the car about a mile away and the cat got out and ran. I lost the cat."

"So far I can honestly say I don't understand the killing part, but it's okay, we're listening."

"Okay so, the cat runs away from me, and I go home. Next morning, the cops are at my door. Turns out the cat jumped through the open window in the kitchen to get back in the house, and when he did that, he hit the burners on the stove, which caused a fire and caused the house to burn down. So, here I am, waking up at my own house after losing a cat, and I am arrested for trying to kill my ex-fiancé in a house fire."

"Well, that is quite a story."

"It's true."

"And here you are."

"And here I am."

These types of conversations happened day in and day out. Whether it was about why someone was in this place or what they did before or what their family was like, we were always trying to get to know each other and be supportive. Certainly not a bunch of hardened criminals by any stretch.

Don't get me wrong, there were some "hardened criminals," but they kept to themselves. Most of those folks did their time in a maximum security facility elsewhere in the state.

At five a.m., a corrections officer would come into the dorm to count us. We were lucky—we always seemed to get the friendly and courteous Ms. Washington, a chubby woman in her thirties with unruly mahogany-brown hair and a ready smile, who bore a strong resemblance to a young Aretha Franklin. If we wanted breakfast, she would invite us—I say, "invite us," because some of the other staff would literally bark orders like a drill sergeant. Ms. Washington simply encouraged us to head over to the kitchen once she'd finished her headcount and swapped a bit of banter with us. Ms. Washington was a light in the dark place I'd found myself, and she brightened up my mornings. But still, I hadn't eaten breakfast since my arrest; it just didn't seem to agree with me anymore. Instead, I found that making hot tea in the dormitory, savoring the peacefulness while most of the other women were in the cafeteria, was the best gift I could give myself.

"Good morning, everyone," Ms. Washington with her trademark wide smile continued. "Those of you who are going to eat breakfast, line up once I've done a quick headcount and we will get moving. Sound good?"

"Yes, ma'am," we resounded, one or two of my cellmates' offering salutes that Ms. Washington seemed to find hilarious.

"Now then, girls," she mock-admonished, "is this jail or boot camp?"

As I'd suspected right from the start, many of these women were victims of circumstance—one young woman had been forced into a trafficking job when she was kidnapped from a date. She hadn't seen her family in years. She had been moved multiple times around the country, and each time she started to figure things out, they would drug her again. Once she was able to become sober enough to realize where she was, she had an escape planned, and that was the day she was arrested.

Another young lady had been taken off the street by a pimp, and ultimately, what she perceived as someone helping her turned into her becoming a hooker and heroin addict, as well as a dealer. Her withdrawal symptoms had been agonizing to watch in the early days—my healing hands had longed to reach out to her, but on day one, *I had decided to be extremely discreet about who I was, and revealing I had a supernatural gift was out of the question.* The poor girl must have gone through a nightmare until the kindly Ms. Washington arranged to have her treated correctly in the hospital wing.

There was also a nun with us who had been fighting for justice when she was arrested for "inciting a riot" outside of a nuclear power plant—she had merely tried to take a stand against militarism and nuclear war and instead ended up being convicted and given a prison sentence. She was challenging the "security state" itself. Her story was one of many that stuck with me.

As for the others, many shared the same response: "I was the victim of a setup." A waitress for a twenty-four-hour diner caught her boss helping himself to the restaurant's profits, only to find herself the one accused of stealing when a wad of cash mysteriously made its way into her purse. There were a few other drug-related "offenses," too, but these people weren't evil. These were not criminals; they were just people worth saving to receive a second chance.

"Hey Ashley," I asked, mixing my tea and hot water. We were the only two who had stayed behind, choosing to forgo breakfast in the cafeteria. "Do you ever think about what Raphael said about archangels?"

"I think about it a lot," she said softly "I am hoping that once we are done with this nightmare, I can get some answers. Nobody in my family ever told me about Uncle So and So, the angel."

"I have questions too, and yeah, I'm right there with you. It's cool though, right?"

"I think so. I guess I don't know what I think until I know more."

"Yeah–agreed. So, hey aside from the 'angel talk,' have you noticed the similarities between many of these girls? They all appear to be highly malleable."

"Malleable?" Ashley asked.

"You know, compliant, easily talked into doing things, following orders, pliable?" I said.

"Oh, yeah, they sure do. They seemed to be smart enough, but it also seems like they could easily be talked into doing almost anything. Like puppets on demand," she said as she tied up her long curly hair, getting ready for a day of work in the landscape crew. "You know what else, Kate? It is amazing to me that there was nobody who would stand up for these people. These people were scared into taking plea deals even when they were innocent. It seemed like nobody cared for these people, and everybody was looking for who to point the finger at, no matter what the situation. The unfairness. The meanness. The downright gall of people. Disgusting."

"I agree. It's hard to just take it in. It goes against everything I believed up until this point in my life."

"I know what you mean."

With that, the doors clicked open, and the dorm was filled with forty-eight other girls all back from breakfast and getting ready for their various work assignments.

Dorms one, two, three, and four were referred to as being "on an island." To get there, we had to cross the main campus, walking away from Dorms *A*, *B*, and *C*—the grim buildings surrounding the courtyard we'd been brought into when we first arrived—and pass the cafeteria, the medical center, and several classrooms where people could work towards receiving their GED. There was also a hair salon where we could get our hair cut every eight weeks for free by someone who knew what she was doing. Crossing the patio and grassy front outside the hair salon led us to the section where we lived.

Our dorm had doors that opened onto a back porch and windows that viewed the field—and most nights, a beautiful sunset. It was more like an honor dorm situation than prison, for sure, but I still didn't want to be there. I was in alignment with Ashley on that: when would this ordeal end?

A few people worked with me in the administration wing—some worked for the warden directly, others worked in intake on the days new people were accepted into the facility, and some worked in the library. The administration was a fully functioning town of its own, no doubt about it. We did a lot of different things, including helping new people get organized, laundry, blanket distribution, allocating clothing, arranging shelves upon shelves of boots, and so on. We did manage to squeeze in a bit of fun, but everyone around me was a hard worker.

We were all just ordinary women—give or take a superpower or two—thrown together by extraordinary circumstances.

To be honest, prison life wasn't all that bad—except the utter lack of freedom. That stunk. Some days in my job (which was Monday through Friday), we had to do a bit of light work, perhaps some cleaning or sewing or a bit of administration, but we were no chain gang. In the afternoons and evenings, there was arts and crafts, maybe some singing—Ms. Washington led the choir, so we all enjoyed those days, and it was good to let off some steam with a valiant attempt at the high notes. Then there were study days when we headed off to the library—that was where I would be when I realized my purpose, my mission, the *WHY* of why I was here in this situation.

That day, as I entered, I saw a familiar, slim, dark-haired figure sitting at a table, engrossed in whatever book she'd chosen to read.

"Hey, Wanda, can I sit here?"

"Yeah, come on."

I liked Wanda. She seemed intelligent and was often found in the library, completing her master's degree in therapeutic movements. The library was in the administration wing where I often worked, too, so we'd gotten to know each other well.

"So listen, Wanda, can I ask you something?" I leaned in to speak quietly. "What work did you do?"

"I was a dance teacher. You know, ballroom, tap, Latin, and so on."

"Wow," I said. "And, if you don't mind me asking–do you have any idea how this place is run? Who manages it? I'm just really curious."

"You might not like the answer, but let me fill you in. The main thing you need to know is this place is a sham. I've been researching this, and I found a journal article by some intrepid reporter named Bill Colosimo from the *Weekly Leader*, it was buried on page twenty-three, but its revelations were shocking." She lowered her voice. "It appears that each person held here is worth one dollar every day. It's a private prison—owned and operated by a corporation that makes money from inmates."

I was stunned. I had never heard of such a thing.

"The more people secured—in other words, locked up—the more funding the prison receives. All paid by the government. The county gets money, too—heck, even the judge and the court officers receive excess in some form or another. It's all about money—kickbacks galore."

My mind was spinning. If I would have heard this a few years ago, I might have dismissed it as hyperbole, but unfortunately, as I would learn, it is an all too real truth of the way the system works in the United States.

"So, who oversees all of this?" I asked.

"I couldn't believe it when I read it for the first time, and I found myself reading it over and over again because it sounded almost made up. According to the article, there's some private company that owns the facility named PLB, LLC, but it's weird—any time I try to locate more information, try to dig further, I hit a brick wall."

The awful truth sunk in. This wasn't about rehabilitation or making the world a better place, or even about keeping "criminals" off the streets. Everything about this operation pointed back to one thing: money.

CHAPTER SIX

"Morning, Ash," I walked over to her after most everyone had left for breakfast.

"Morning." Her eyes dulled with no sign of the sparkle I had come to appreciate.

"It's Saturday!" I tried to sound cheery and boost her spirits. It didn't work. The cloud above Ashley's head was darker than the one that accompanied Herman Munster's car in the old black and white episodes of *The Munsters*. I smiled as I remembered watching those reruns on Saturday mornings as a child.

"So, what have you got planned for today?" I asked in my brightest voice.

With a loud huff, Ashley turned watery eyes in my direction. "Kathryn, when is this nightmare going to end?"

"I don't know. We still have to figure out why we are here, what the true reason is."

"I am sick and tired of being treated this way and being away from everybody, from my life. Last night was the worst. The fact that the guards came in, woke us all up, and shuttled us into the gym was bad enough, but . . ." and her voice trailed off. I knew what she was going to say though. Last night the guards raided the dorm. During a middle-of-the-night raid, the lights blast on, everybody jumps off their bunks, and no matter what you have on, you are lined up and sent to the gym. There, each girl is stripped naked and "checked." Meanwhile, back at the dorm, lockers are being tossed, mattresses flipped upside down, it's a nightmare.

"I didn't get any sleep after that," I said to her. "I was able to get my bed remade, but my locker stuff is everywhere, and I really felt attacked."

"Yeah, me too. When is this going to end?" She shook her head, her long hair frizzing out from lack of nutrients. "You know what, Kathryn, I'm a good person," Ashley went on. "This experience has opened my eyes to the lack of justice in the 'justice' system. Do you have any idea how many times I have heard, 'And the DA and judge told me they would make an example of me'? That's a big part of the reason these women believe they're here! Nobody is ever going to look up who was 'made an example of' to find out if they deserved it. It's just wrong."

"Yeah, I get what you're saying, but honestly, I have no idea what the next step is," I shrugged, helpless.

The women began to file back into the dormitory.

"Well, that was a quick breakfast," I exclaimed out loud to no one in particular.

"Breakfast was awful as ever, Kathryn, but honestly we are all too exhausted to even care," Christina responded. "I know somebody who works in the kitchen, and they don't give them the right ingredients or tools to actually make decent meals. If they did, imagine how that would turn things around."

"You're probably right." Scrap probably from that sentence—Christina was a genius with food.

"Hey, do you want to make dinner tonight? I'm thinking tuna wraps with cheese," she said with a twinkle in her eye. My heart lifted, and the Herman Munster car cloud above Ashley's head started to clear. Even with minimal ingredients, Christina was a creative cook. The commissary offered us things like cheese puffs, ramen noodles, and tuna, and a good trick that she had developed was to take the flat iron that people used to straighten their hair and fill a tortilla wrap with tuna and noodles or sauce, wrap that in a piece of paper, and "toast" it. I didn't know what to think until I tried it, and then I never questioned it again—it was miraculous.

"Watch out, coming through!" Two female officers walked into the dorm and dropped off a young woman. "Ladies, please welcome Annabelle Montblanc." Their voices were crass, and the word "ladies" was slanged with insult.

What a name! I thought. It sounded made up. Annabelle was tall, probably five feet nine or five feet ten, and slender. She had perfect teeth (possibly fake), seemed like the type of person that worked out every day, and exuded an air of affluence. She was clearly out of her element. Her hair was almost platinum with an undertone of blonde, something very trendy, but also very expensive at the salon.

As most new inmates do for the first few days, Annabelle was crying, and we all knew just to let her get it out.

We had an interesting process we used with each and every new arrival: one by one, the other women around me grabbed something from their locker, brought it to her bunk, introduced themselves with a hug or a smile, and gave her the items. Hot chocolate, tea, crackers, peanut butter—you name it. Like a neighborhood welcoming committee. This was how we took care of each other. She had nothing, and wouldn't for several weeks, and the girls in this dormitory knew it—and thought nothing of sharing.

Our dorm was the only dorm that did this for people – other dorms had issues with theft of food from lockers, and "snitching"–things like a woman whispering to a guard, "Oh, you need to check her locker, she has peanut butter from the kitchen . . ." and then bam, chaos broke out. But not our dorm. We were lucky.

Finally she raised her head, dark eyes still swimming with tear residue, and out came a meek voice. "Hey, call me AB."

"I'm Kathryn."

"Are you on outside detail?"

"No, I work in administration. Did they put you on outside detail?"

"Yeah, Parks."

"Not bad. My friend Ashley is on Parks. It's a good gig."

She just looked down at the floor.

"Anyway, welcome to Dorm One. We call it summer camp."

I caught a glimpse of a full sleeve of tattoo art on AB's arm. But not just any tattoos, interwoven among them was an eyeball, one that closely resembled the secreto spectrum regale.

Later, I nudged Ashley. "She has the mark."

"Is she one of us?" Ashley leaned in closer so that the others wouldn't hear.

"I don't think so, but she absolutely has the mark."

"Well, it's not exactly like ours, but its close. The eyeball was the same, but there was no scepter going through it."

"No scepter? I wonder what that means." Ashley replied thoughtfully.

I also wondered—was there a similar mark that was not angelic?

CHAPTER SEVEN

When you have been 'inside' for a while, you forget about the rest of the world.

College and the daily grind of the HGS felt like distant memories—like someone else's memories. Being in prison was like living in an alternate universe.

I was waiting in a dull hallway in the administration wing with three other women, and I was numb. Yes, I would smile and be polite, but I had learned that in order to survive I had to put myself into a protective state, leaving me numb to the world, as a way to manage the experience.

"It's going to be a busy day today!" Ms. Washington exclaimed as she walked into the office and switched on the lights. "Have you been waiting long?" she called into the hallway, where we had been sitting for twenty minutes. We hoped to get a jump on the maintenance and laundry, but there was nobody who could find a key to the room. Hard to believe, but that was what we had been told.

"No one to find a key. What's wrong with these people? They all know the keys' location, and they all know you were each chosen to work in admin because you set the bar for everyone. There should be no issue in letting you inside. I'll have to talk to them later."

Within moments, the doors were unlocked, and our workday began.

"As much as I hate being locked up, at least we have this work detail. Better than just sitting around. It helps pass the time," I said to nobody in particular.

"Hey, what's that?" Caprice pointed to what looked like a small lightbulb in the corner.

"It looks like a camera, but it's pretty well hidden," I explained. "Last week, the maintenance workers took that shelving unit down over there, so it must have been there all along, just hidden."

"Huh? Hey, Ms. Washington, is this active? Are we being spied on?" Caprice yelled. That was just her style—she would blurt out whatever was on her mind, but we never took offense. It was just Caprice being Caprice. She was short, but powerful.

"What's that, Caprice?" Ms. Washington entered the laundry room, peering at the newly revealed camera. "Oh yeah, we used to use that security system, but somebody installed new systems along the way. I guess someone forgot about removing that camera. I wonder if it's still active or not—Kathryn, would you mind checking?"

I was surprised she'd asked me to have a look. After all, I was a prisoner—a falsely accused one, but a prisoner nonetheless—and she was asking me to check out the security! I wasn't going to refuse. I liked Ms. Washington. In fact, I felt totally and completely at ease with her around, like nothing terrible could happen while she was there.

"Hey, Caprice, give me that chair." I reached over, grabbing the top rung and pulling the chair towards me.

"Why do you need a chair? Oh, never mind, I probably know better than to ask questions at this point, right? Right!"

I climbed up and untwisted the glass ball. There was a spot where an old camera used to be, but not anymore. Instead, I saw a small box with a button on the top and a note that read, KATHRYN, PUSH ME. I blinked. Did that really have a message for me?

I grabbed the note and squirreled it away in my pocket, figuring I would push the button later and then put the glass ball back into place.

"Nothing here. Just dust," I said, climbing back down. "Hey, girls, I gotta go to the bathroom."

Moments later, I closed the bathroom door behind me and took the box out of my pocket. Inside was a handwritten note from Raphael.

Dear Kathryn,

By now, you know that this is more than just a regular mission. You have come face to face with systemic injustice and have seen how the system ensnares innocent people, yourself included. You have surely seen by now that there are many other women with you who do not deserve to be there.

The PLB, LLC group that runs your facility also oversees a men's facility as well. The entire PLB is run by the Paolucci family. The mob. And your aunt, Jacquelyn Paolucci, has agents working inside your jail.

Your mission is to identify the insiders so we can find and stop her before she has the chance to recruit any more people for her cause. They prey on the prison population because many are desperate, impressionable, and will do anything to free themselves.

I trust you and Ashley are both holding up. Watch and be aware— Barry will be rotating into the scene as well. Try not to react when you see him, but know he is there for your safety and security. Let's focus on stopping Jacquelyn and her attempt at world domination once and for all. I have told Scott that you are safe and explained this to him, so he understands the mission from a high level.
Best,

Raphael

And that was all. I must have read the letter ten times before it sank in that even in this hidden note—the one that Raphael had gone to so much trouble to place so that I would find it—he still hadn't given me much insight on the how or why of the mission. But at least now I knew something, and knowing something was better than knowing nothing.

I couldn't wait to get back to the dorm and tell Ashley, but I still had five hours of work ahead of me.

"Hey, Kathryn, are you ready to eat?" Christina grabbed my arm, almost giddy with excitement. "Wait until you see what I did." Christina, who wore her long hair in a ponytail and had an eager smile, could make anybody feel at ease. I really appreciated that about her. She never spoke much about why she was here, but supposedly it saved her life by getting her out of a worse situation back home.

I headed to one of the tables in the common area. There, she had laid out napkins and wraps in bowls, and—wait a minute, was that a cake?

"Come on, now, a cake? For real?" I asked.

"I made it out of . . . well, let's just say I had to take apart some snack cakes and cobble it together, but I think it is going to be great. We have enough for one more, do you want me to go ask Ashley if she wants to come eat with us?"

Ashley was the only other woman who remained in the dorm until all the others had gone to the dining hall. Their loss—I always opted to stay in the dorm, especially when Christina was making food.

"Yeah, great idea. The more, the merrier."

As the three of us sat down and discussed our days, it was almost normal. The placidness of the room made it seem like we were somewhere else. We had a moment to breathe, and we relished it. We feasted on Christina's magical food extravaganza. I never knew someone could do so much with minimal ingredients. Wow. The cake helped create a festive atmosphere, and as the other women filtered back in, our laughter brought them over. No one wanted to miss out.

"Hey!" AB yelled, walking straight towards our table from the doorway as Ashley scooped up the last remaining crumbs with her fingertips.

"You guys had cake and didn't share? Way out of line," she said sarcastically. Since her unhappy arrival a month or so ago, AB had fit in well with the rest of the women in Dorm One, being a friendly person with a great sense of humor. If there was a funny side to be seen in any situation, you could bet AB would find it, and we'd all enjoyed a lot more laughter since she'd joined us. That was the joy of the evening together —lots of laughter and the camaraderie of people who had decided to make the most of a difficult situation, together.

It was a happy moment in a sad place, but I was aware I had work to do. So did Ashley, but she didn't know it yet.

"Hey, Ash," I whispered as the impromptu dinner started to break up, and the women around us headed back to their beds. "If you have a minute, can I talk to you?"

"Yeah, sure," running a hand through her long curls as we sat side by side on her bunk. Thankfully, this wasn't the sort of facility that required we all cut our hair—Ashley would have been devastated to have lost her beautiful blonde locks. We just had to always keep it up off of our shoulders, so we had a ton of hairbands to do just that.

"I found a secret note from Raphael."

"A secret note?" Ashley leaned in closer. "How secret could it be if you found it?"

"I found it hidden in the laundry. I have no idea how long it had been there or how he knew I would be the one to find it. Regardless, get this. The owners of this prison—PLB, LLC—is an arm of the Paolucci family."

Ashley stared as if trying to process what I was saying.

"And Jacquelyn is still trying to wreak havoc on the world."

"Wow, she really has a thing about world domination, doesn't she?"

"Jacquelyn has agents inside; our mission is to oust them and sabotage their operations. They're using the inmates for recruiting. Look out for anything unusual—you know the deal."

"Okay."

"Oh, and one more thing before I go. Raphael noted that Barry would be infiltrating the prison somehow, and we're not to react in any way that could give him away when we see him."

"Huh, why Barry? Why not Mike or Greg?" Ashley's voice grew wistful when she spoke Greg's name, and I squeezed her hand. I got it. She missed him, just like I missed Scott, even if she and Greg weren't officially in a relationship. I'd realized long ago they had feelings for each other—I'd be blind not to.

"I guess there's a chance Jacquelyn would recognize Michael or Greg." To me, Michael had never been "Mike" as he was to Ashley and Greg. I was more old school—like Raphael was.

"Geez! Do you think Jacquelyn's in here? I mean, somewhere in this same facility. Wouldn't we recognize her?"

"Don't forget she can shapeshift," I whispered with a shudder. "According to Raphael, it's more likely she's got agents in here, recruiting, and it's our job to stop that. Unrecruit her recruits or something like that."

"How do we do that?"

I grinned. "What do we always do? We wing it, of course."

CHAPTER EIGHT

The days tended to blur together in prison; however, weekends made up for it. On the weekends, visitors could come into the facility. You could spend all day talking with your visitor, well from 9:00 a.m. until 3:00 p.m. There was usually a "bathroom break" in the middle where all of the prisoners would line up and be escorted to a bathroom and then back to the visitation room. The visitors could also use the vending machine to purchase drinks or snacks that you could share. (Inmates were not allowed to go near the vending machines–another one of those rules I never understood.) I guess the ultimate job of a guard, even at a 'low to medium security center,' was to make the experience as difficult as possible for everyone involved.

Visitations were based on your last name, so *A-K* on one day and *L-Z* on the other day.

Sunday was my day.

Walking eagerly across the campus, I was excited. It was kind of cold, but I wore my thermal under my short sleeve shirt.

As I headed down the hall towards the visitors' area, I spotted Scott waiting for me. I was overjoyed. A quick exchange with the guard on duty, sign into the book, and then it was just me and Scott for the next few hours.

The visitor's area reminded me of an old elementary cafeteria. The walls were painted with inspirational quotes and a forest scene, and there were vending machines filled with snacks, sandwiches, and drinks. When a visitor arrived, they came in and sat down in a folding chair that faced another chair and had to wait until the person they were visiting arrived. Then, and only then, could you stand up, hug, and then sit down. No real displays of affection, maybe a quick kiss, but only if nobody saw you. If a guard saw behavior they didn't like, they could kick your visitor out and stop your "visitation privileges," so people really tried to behave.

"Wow," he stammered. "It's . . . wow." Scott was overcome with joy, tears, and frustration; all the emotions that had been boiling up since the last time we saw each other. "It is really great to see you, Cinnamon." And with that, he threw his arms around me, engulfing me in a giant hug.

My body shook, and I couldn't seem to control my response. My arms were twitching, and I felt goosebumps all over. I was hot and cold at the same time. It was a full-on physical parasympathetic reaction to almost coming out of the 'daily' that had been my life behind these walls. I missed him so very much and I hated this so much and it was as if my body was expressing everything I couldn't say with words.

"I'm . . . sorry," is all I could manage.

"Sorry? For what?"

"This is awful. I don't know what to do. I don't know what happened. I don't . . ." and I stopped. My initial burst of glee gave way to a nauseous, clammy feeling. Scott's presence made me yearn so desperately for life on the outside. For my life.

"Let's sit down and breathe." Scott gently waited until I sat in the chair across from him. "This is not easy, but we will get through it," he reassured me, even though I could tell he was crumbling inside.

"Have you had any luck figuring out why I'm here?" I was working hard, trying to hold down my fury.

"It's awful, and I know you didn't do anything wrong. The judge who denied you bail is corrupt—and we're certain, on the take. That's how they can cram so many people in this place without due process. The whole system is so crooked, and even trying to get in front of someone who may be able to help costs money and time, so I'm doing what I can, but they make money every day you are here, so they have no incentive to act."

Scott's face showed exhaustion and sadness, and he was doing his best to hold it together for me.

"So I learned something too about why I'm here . . ." I was reluctant to speak candidly. There were dozens of inmates and visitors in the room, along with hawk-eyed guards, and I worried about anyone overhearing what I was about to share.

"Oh, I have so much to tell you, but there is never enough time—and certainly not enough privacy to go through it all. Did you talk to Raphael?"

"Well, I am going to try and listen as best I can. I miss you so much." He began to get choked up. "And, yes, I talked to Raphael, and I do understand from a high level so there is no need to talk about that now. And I know what was in the letter, okay? Musa and I were with Raphael when he wrote it. He wanted our input."

Phew. What a relief.

"Let's just enjoy our time together and try and be thankful for this moment," I said. My voice quavered as I tried to be strong.

"You're right," Scott whispered, taking out his handkerchief and dabbing at the corners of his eyes. "Can I grab you a drink, or a sandwich, or?"

"Yeah, a soda pop would be nice—maybe a ginger ale?"

"Ginger ale it is, then tell me what's been happening. Fill me in."

And fill him in I did. I explained about the dorms, and the other women, and rec time (which was anything from girls lying out in the sun to a pickup softball game). He joked that it seemed like summer camp without a swimming pool.

"Looks like I haven't got any news about you though. What've you been doing?" I asked.

"Oh, this and that," Scott seemed intentionally vague. "Here and now isn't a good place to discuss it. But I am more involved than I ever was, and I am so very proud of you."

Scott glanced at the clock on the wall. "Our time is ticking away. So, how do you feel about attending Mass?"

"How do I feel about what?" I said, totally wrong-footed by the conversation's change in direction.

"Mass. You know, candles, incense, Hail Mary's, the Pope . . ."

"The Pope's coming to prison in Alaska to hold Mass?"

Scott laughed. "No, silly. Well, kind of, actually," he added cryptically. "I hear there's a new priest in town, and he's good. You'll love him."

"Scott, I'm not even Roman Catholic."

"Just go," he said. "Oh and be sure to take Ashley with you."

"Ashley is Baptist."

"You'll understand soon enough. There'll be a Mass this afternoon, five o'clock sharp. Not long to go, so you'd better hurry up after we are done. Find Ashley, and be sure and get them to sign you out for Mass."

"I really don't know what you're up to, but I guess it is the same God for everyone so this could be good for us. Plus it gets us out of the dorm."

Scott just grinned irritatingly back at me, and with that, the bell went off and the announcement was made: "Visitation is ending, please say good-bye and make your way to the exit. Inmates, remain in your seats until all visitors have cleared the room."

Walking back into the dorm, I didn't even stop but rather went straight to Ashley's bunk. "Hey Ash, Catholic Mass is going to be at 5:00 p.m., do you want to go with me?"

"Kate, I'm Baptist, you know that."

"Just being in church might be good for both of us," I said.

"Why not?"

They had set up metal folding chairs in the visitation area, with a table in front serving as the altar. We picked two seats in the front row, facing the big table. There were dozens of women here; the room was full. A female corrections officer walked in accompanying a man in robes.

"Everyone, this is Deacon Jerry, and he is going to be performing Mass today, and possibly in the coming weeks, so treat him nicely." The guard chuckled, and the deacon stood quietly smiling beside her.

The guard left, and Deacon Jerry took his place beside the makeshift altar. He looked me squarely in the eye and winked. Then, he smiled at Ashley. BAM! The man we knew as Barry Pope—ah, very funny, Scott, of course the "Pope" was coming—was standing in front of us.

Barry—I mean, Deacon Jerry—passed out bulletins, and everyone took their seats. He began with some announcements, including the fact that this week, as he was new to us, he would be taking confession from anyone who needed it every week before the service began.

"It'll give me a chance to get to know you all a bit more too," he intoned. Genius! He had contrived an opportunity for Ashley and me to speak to him in private.

Without missing a beat, Barry segued effortlessly into an introductory prayer, then gave a short sermon on the topic of finding ourselves in the strangest of places and still believing in God. Very appropriate, particularly for Ashley and myself.

"Hey, Kathryn, look," Ashley whispered, leaning over, and showing me a communication earpiece inside of her bulletin. She turned and pretended to tousle her hair, quickly inserting the earpiece at the same time. Looking in my bulletin, I saw that there was one for me too.

We each quickly tugged at our hair and swept it back over our ear, while sliding the earwig into place.

"Hey, guys." Greg's voice spoke in our ears, and it was all I could do to stop myself from turning to look at Ashley. "I know you can't respond to me, but I can see you are both online and have your earpieces in. This just highlights what I had known all along—everything is working, and Barry has gotten to you both.

"We have quite a mission ahead of us. Jacquelyn has reinvented herself as the head of PLB, LLC, the private-sector owner and operator of several women's jails and low-security prison facilities. She is trying to recruit people from inside, and it's been working. She sneaks twenty or so women out every month, and they go to work for her in one of her underground operations. Meanwhile, one of her goals is to run the entire jail system and then run for office on the platform of 'prison reform.' Of course, we know it's all a sham. Reform? Jacquelyn? Ha!" He chuckled mirthlessly. "I won't be talking to you all the time—you'll have to leave the earpieces in the bulletins and hand them back to Barry at the end of Mass, I'm afraid—but I will let you know through him whatever I see and hear on the outside. Make sure you attend confession."

"Between my input and spiritual guidance from 'Deacon Barry,' I hope this gives you guys a little support. We miss you here."

That was all we heard.

After the service, as we walked back to the dormitory, Ashley scooted up next to me in line.

"What are we supposed to do with the information Greg told us?" she whispered.

"I don't know yet, Ashley. Let's both think about it. If we put our heads together, we can figure out the next moves and how we can support this mission."

There we were, thinking on our feet. It reminded me of the good old days, out in the field with the rest of the team.

"Hey, Kathryn, wait!" Christina yelled, running up behind us. "Great service, huh? And I love my rosary. I've never had a rosary before, and I like the idea of having something that is a constant reminder about God and the universe and, well you know, all the things."

"Yeah, it's great to have that while we are in here," I said. "I didn't know you were Catholic."

"I was raised with just a hodgepodge of stuff, but I really like the Catholic beliefs, and I want to pursue this so this is the perfect timing for me, even though I've never been much of a religious person. After hearing Deacon Jerry, I sure want to know more. He excited my heart, and I haven't felt that in a long time."

"Wow, that's great, Christina." I was really happy when one of the girls had something touching happen to them. It was hard enough living through this for each of us, and any bit of light I tried to celebrate no matter if it was me or someone else.

"No, wait, there's more," she could hardly contain herself. "As I was leaving the church—I mean, the meeting room, but it's always going to be a church to me now . . . not that I'll be here much longer . . ." Christina jumped up and down and clapped her hands with glee, and Ashley and I couldn't help but smile at her euphoria.

"You are getting out soon?" Ashley leaned in, suddenly very interested in the conversation. "That's the best news, although I'll sure miss your toasted tortillas."

"Yeah, I am so into God right now, I could burst. Back there at Mass, I prayed for a way out of this place, and d'you know what? He answered my prayer, like, right away. I always thought you had to pray and pray for ages, but now, God's on it."

"What are you talking about?" I asked.

"I was leaving Mass when Ms. Jerilyn caught my arm. You know, she oversees physical training?"

I only knew Ms. Jerilyn by sight—a skinny peroxide blonde whose habit of scraping her hair away from her face into a tight ponytail only served to make her angular features appear even sharper. At six feet, Christina was the star of the prison women's basketball team, so she knew Ms. Jerilyn better than me.

"Anyhow, she stopped me and asked me if I'd be interested in an opportunity to secure my future. She explained to us that I might be paroled! I'd have to do a work-release program, but they have an opening for a chef in their headquarters!"

"Who is they?" I asked.

"PLB. The company that runs the prison, apparently."

So that was it. Jacquelyn's plan in action. But what was her goal with the prisoners? Certainly not to train the next generation of short-order cooks. It wasn't clear yet.

"I'm not supposed to discuss this with anyone, but I figure if I can't trust you guys, I can't trust anyone."

Everyone trusts Ashley, I thought, realizing her clairsentience would be helpful. No way were we going to let Christina fall into Jacquelyn's clutches, only to be used and abused, then left in the trash—or worse. If anyone could persuade her that her "dream opportunity" was a terrible idea, Ashley could.

"Ms. Jerilyn believes that I'm a victim, that I should never have been here in the first place. Apparently, the head of the corporation came across my case file and decided to intervene. At last, someone believes me."

"Have you met her? The top woman, I mean," I asked.

"Of course not," replied Christina. "She's a busy and powerful woman, and I'll be honored to work for her . . ." Christina trailed off as she realized she was hardly getting the whoops of joy she'd been expecting from us.

"What is it?" she asked, as Ashley and I looked at each other, Ashley giving me the ghost of a nod to let me know she had a plan. "Aren't you happy for me? I'm sure I can put a good word in for you too."

Ashley put a comforting arm around Christina, and I just had time to hear her murmur, "You know, when something seems too good to be true, it often is, but don't be upset—I've got a better idea . . ."

"I don't understand," she said.

"You don't have to understand right now. Just think about this and try and find out more information," I said.

Back in Dorm One, I hadn't even gotten to my bunk when Wanda, whom I knew well from our months of working together in admin, ran up to me.

"Hey, Kathryn, can I ask you something?"

"Sure, what's up?"

"Have you heard of the PLB group that owns this place?"

Oh no, not Wanda too.

"Well, Ms. Clare pulled me aside earlier and asked if I would be interested in getting out earlier than planned and working for them as a fashion designer. I mean, what does a group that owns prisons need with a fashion designer? Like, seriously? Unless they've got interests in more than one sector. So, I can get out of here and have my dream job—I told her I would have to think about it, but it sounds exciting, right?"

I was pleased to hear that Wanda seemed a little skeptical of the offer.

"Hey Wanda, what is your gut telling you? It doesn't sound like it's on the up and up, does it?"

"Well, at this point, I feel like nobody in power wants to help me, and everybody is corrupt, so the fact that someone took an interest in me and asked about me and wants to help me has got to be important." She eyed me warily, seeing right through my unease. "So, what's bugging you about this?"

"I think you need to be asking yourself what's bugging *you* about this, but to me, it doesn't feel right. If you want to do it, then all I ask is that you keep your eyes open and watch your back."

Wanda looked at me, her fingers twisting her bottom lip, her face expressionless. Finally, she replied. "I hear you, Kathryn. I felt there was something odd about this—you know, too good to be true."

"Well, my advice would be to follow your instincts." Then, I took a risk and decided to share an idea I'd hardly had time to consider myself. What was it, a premonition? Did I have that gift? Hadn't I dreamed I would end up in this very prison, way back in New York, in the brownstone, with Scott? That fantastic night we got married.

Pull yourself together, Kathryn.

I cleared my throat and obeyed my inner voice. No use moping about the past when I had a job to do. A vitally important job.

Yet.

"You know, I think we'll be getting out of here soon, one way or another. Don't ask me how. Just trust me."

Wanda regarded me with her familiar steady gaze. I could see the trust in her eyes. Then she spoke.

"You got it."

The words gave me all the encouragement I needed to see my mission through completion.

Wanda's gaze shifted to a woman approaching us. She was loud, but she was kind. She was bubbly, but sometimes had no filter. This was Caprice.

"Hey Katherine, hey Wanda. What are you guys up to?"

"Nothing much, you?"

"Well, just thinking about how soon I can get out of this place. I spoke to my lawyer, she's working on some filings. Fingers crossed I should be out very soon—after all, my family needs me."

"Caprice, how big is your family?" I asked.

"I have two boys and a girl, and two turtles and three cats. Oh yeah, and one elderly aunt. My aunt is taking care of everything while I'm going through this, bless her heart, but she can't do that forever—she's almost eighty!"

"Wow, that's quite a bit. Were you married, or . . .?"

"I was married, but after the third child was born, he decided it was too stressful for him, and he left. Just left. No divorce, no nothing—just gone—poof!" She shook her head as if she could see him right there in front of her.

"Wow, I'm sad to hear that, but you sound like you're doing okay."

"Okay? I'm better than okay. You know I'm a dancer, and I make no less than $5,000 a week doing what I do, which gives me time with my family and the ability to pay our bills."

"What kind of dancing do you do?" Wanda asked.

"Exotic. I don't strip, I just dance."

Wanda's eyes widened and she let out a soft, "Huh."

"It's a good living, and usually it's pretty safe . . . but as you can see, I'm in here with you ladies, which means something went wrong—and boy, was it wrong. I trusted the wrong man."

"That's a common story among many of us," Wanda said.

"Well, keep us posted on your lawyer," I said. "We hope you can get home to your family soon."

"Yeah, I'll see you ladies around." She twisted her entire body, then snapped her head and said, "This is how we exit in the dancing biz," and with a smile and a fresh dose of bubbly personality, she was off.

"Hey, Wanda?"

"Huh?"

"Sometimes I can't believe the type of people that are here. It's baffling to me," I said.

"Yeah, I've stopped trying to figure it out—it's just humans, and corruption, and honestly there are so many things broken about the justice system. At the end of the day, there is no justice, there is 'just us,' so we are doing the best we can with what we've got."

"'Just us.' Brilliant . . . that is brilliant," I said, mulling the bitter but undeniable truth of her words.

When I got back to my bunk, I tried to relax. I made a cup of tea and put in my earbuds to listen to the radio. Within a few moments, though, Ashley was over the other side of the bunk, poking at me.

"Guess what? Guess what? Today I was out on my work assignment. We were doing landscaping in town, and on our lunch break, I saw Greg!"

"Did you talk to him?"

"No, but he motioned me to a particular area, and as we left, I noticed a letter there, so I picked it up and brought it back with me." She handed over the scrunched-up envelope.

There was only one way to get contraband like this inside the prison. I looked at Ashley, aghast. "You brought it back with you? Ewww!"

"It's the only way to get anything back in, and you know that. It's not pretty, but I did it."

"You stuffed it into your pocketbook?" I asked, raising my eyebrows.

"Sure, if that's what you want to call the secret compartment that I had to hide it in. I put it into a Ziploc bag first, so don't worry. You're not touching anything weird."

"Oh. Okay. You didn't read it?"

"I figured we should look at it together."

I opened the envelope gently. It appeared to have been through a rough day. The note inside was handwritten:

I know this is hard but hang in there.
Jacquelyn has reappeared, and that is what we were hoping would happen.
Be prepared to take her down at a moments notice.
I am proud of you for sacrificing yourselves.

Michael

"Sacrificing ourselves? What does that mean?" Ashley looked at me like I should have the answers.

"I have no idea."

"I feel like we are two fairly smart, strong women. Why do we have to wait? This undercover stuff can be challenging some days, you know?"

"What is important is that Jacquelyn's undercover operatives have already suggested to several women that they can get out of here and have a dream job with her. She's been doing her homework—dressmaking for Wanda, head chef for Christina. The offer is freedom, but they will never get the freedom or the career—it's just a lie. What do you think Jacquelyn's plan is?"

Ashley shrugged. "You know all the horrible things Jacquelyn has her fingers in. Maybe she'll send them off to sex trafficking. Maybe she'll get them addicted to drugs and force them to do hard labor. Maybe . . ."

Ashley's voice faded from my awareness as I got lost in my thoughts, wondering at all the abominable things Jacquelyn probably had in store for these women. I suppressed a shudder. "We must make sure no one agrees to go, as much as we can. By the way, how did it go with Christina?"

"Good. I feel like the woman is inclined to trust me. She was disappointed, but something delicious will happen soon. I just hope Raphael and the team have something up their sleeves because I like Chris, and I don't want to break that promise."

No. Neither did I.

"Kathryn, Kathryn, come on . . . wake up," Ashley shook me by the shoulders.

It was the next morning. I had overslept—something I never do. Ashley had gotten up on her own.

"What happened to you? After dinner, you went to sleep. You were out like a light."

"I was just exhausted. I think everything hit me at once. I feel better today, though. Thanks for waking me up."

The morning was like every other morning we had experienced since arriving in this odd place. A city unto itself with its eating places, houses, and landscaped yards was an alternative reality. I signed out, greeted the staff as I passed by, and walked to the administration block when Pauline pulled me aside.

"Hey, Kathryn, can I ask you about something?"

"Sure, Pauline, what's going on?"

"Well, last night, one of the guards, Ms. Clare—you know, the tall woman with the poufy blonde hair that looks like a wig, who oversees arts and crafts activities—she came and asked me if I would be interested in considering a way to get out of here sooner, and I was like, 'Are you kidding?' She told me, 'I've got the perfect job for you, and if you accept, it will get you out of here, probably within seventy-two hours or less. She told me to meet her tonight, a half hour after lights out—a bunch of people specifically chosen will be gathering. We will pretty much leave straightaway, and then I will be set up with a job and a place to live and—"

"Pauline, stop. You know this doesn't sound right, don't you? Tell me more about this. When exactly did this happen?"

Pauline blinked. "She talked to me last night, but this is in the works for tonight. Why? Do you want to join us? I'm excited about this, and I can't believe I am one of the chosen few. Ms. Clare told me not to talk about it to anyone, but I figured—well, you aren't just anyone, you're Kathryn, and I value your opinion and friendship."

"That's awfully kind of you, Pauline, but . . . do you think this is the right choice for you?"

"What do you mean?" Pauline answered gruffly, her demeanor turning from excited to angry in a flash. I loved Pauline's company—she was strong-minded, honest, and humorous, but she sure needed to keep a check on that fiery temper of hers. "What is it with you, Kathryn? I thought you'd be pleased for me, but you're way too negative. It's a way out for me, so why shouldn't I take it?"

"Pauline, listen. I'm not trying to bring you down—believe me, I want the best for you. I just don't trust this too-good-to-be-true offer—and yeah, I've heard about it from a few of the others. Before you make up your mind, please, I beg you, go speak to Ashley about it."

"Why? What does Ashley know that I don't?"

"It'll sound better coming from her," I was feeling slightly guilty for dumping this on Ashley but was convinced she could handle it a lot better than I could. "Whatever you decide to do, Pauline, be careful."

So, it was to be tonight.

I hadn't even turned around to get the daily work journals when Caprice grabbed me.

"Hey, Kathryn, do you have a sec?"

"Yeah—I need to get the journal tracking work done, but what's going on? Problems with the intake or supplies or something?"

"No but listen. Let's go into the library where it's quieter, and we can talk for a minute."

The library was a quick walk down the main hall, and we could pretty much come and go as we pleased since we worked in the area. We headed to the back corner and sat down at the study table.

"Everything okay?"

"Yeah . . . So, I'm not supposed to talk to anyone about what I'm about to tell you, but I need some guidance."

Oh no, I felt it coming. Not another one—not another potential recruit. Not Caprice—loud, blunt, loveable Caprice who wouldn't ever dream of hurting anyone.

"Okay, spill."

"Last night, I was in the gym playing a pickup basketball game after dinner—I might be little, but I sure can jump. Anyhoo, Ms. Jerilyn blew the whistle and told everybody to take a break. When I went to grab my water bottle, she followed me and asked if we could talk. I said sure, and she asked me if I wanted to be part of a sure thing. I said that I was trying to move through this to go back to a good life, and I didn't want to be involved in any funny business. She told me that if I decide that I want out of this place, I can meet her tonight on the commons lawn with a bunch of others who were selected, and we will be released and have jobs and places to live and . . ."

Was there a sign on my forehead: Come tell me about the pending disaster? At least I now knew the when and the where. All I needed was a way to stop it.

"Caprice, this is not a good idea," I said shortly, impatience getting the better of me. Not impatience at Caprice, but Jacquelyn—my wretched, evil aunt—and Ms. Clare and Ms. Jerilyn, and all the other people so blinded by their greed that they would gladly do her dirty work for her.

"Do you already know about it? Wait—are you a chosen one too?" Caprice asked, her eyes blazing with excitement.

"No, I'm not a 'chosen one,' but I do know a little about what's going on—I've heard rumblings, and this is not the right choice. They are lying to you; it's not what it seems. I can't stop you, but I can tell you that I sure wish you wouldn't do it."

"Huh?"

"She's right."

I was so engrossed in trying to make Caprice be sensible, I hadn't noticed Wanda come up behind us, and I nearly jumped a foot when she spoke.

"Ms. Clare had a word with me last night about this . . . um, sure thing." Wanda's voice oozed sarcasm when she said sure thing. She was one bright lady. "The 'head of PLB' was looking for someone just like me. I don't know; I switched off as soon as she mentioned that company because I'm telling you now that there is something wrong. The whole thing stinks worse than rotten fish."

Caprice was staring at Wanda, her mouth open. I could hardly contain my grin. Most people who knew Wanda respected her and took her word as gospel, and I knew Caprice seriously looked up to her.

"Well, uh, well . . ."

"Wanda's right, Caprice," I whispered, aware that someone else had come into the library, but not wanting to turn to see who it was. "And there is another way . . ."

"Hi, Ms. Washington," said Wanda brightly, placing her books on the table and sitting down. Although I didn't think that the lovely Ms. Washington was one of Jacquelyn's agents, I wasn't about to take any chances and followed Wanda's lead.

"C'mon, Caprice," I said as casually as I could, "we got to get back to work. Today's a hectic day, and all I want to do is finish up so I can head back to the dorm and take a hot shower. That is, if you don't need anything else?"

"No, I'm good. See you later, Wanda." As we left the room, Caprice grabbed my arm and whispered, "Thanks for listening to me, and thanks for your honesty. If you and Wanda both feel that strongly about this, you must have your reasons. So, I'll think about it, okay?"

"Just be safe and make the right choice, okay? You and me—well, we're friends. Good friends. I'd trust you with my life, and I don't wanna lose you."

Caprice clutched me in a bone-crushing hug. "You won't."

So, there it was. Tonight was the night. How could Ashley and I stop this from happening? We couldn't hope to get to all the women they tried to recruit and persuade them they were walking into a disaster, so what could we do?

An idea came to mind. Oh, this was too good—too perfect. I'd got it. It might not stop Jacquelyn's little game entirely, but it would buy us a few extra valuable hours, at least.

It was time to go to confession.

CHAPTER NINE

"Forgive me, Father, for I have sinned."

I sat in a makeshift confessional, a flimsy wooden booth that looked like it had been cobbled together in a hurry, with a cubicle containing a wooden chair for me—the confessor—and another, I assumed with a similar chair, for Barry. It did at least afford us the privacy we needed; there were guards in the meeting room, but they remained a polite distance away as I whispered my sins through the small hatch connecting the two cubicles.

"It's to be tonight—the breakout, that is," I told Barry in a low voice. "She's promising people a way out of this mess. Clean record, cleared of all charges, that sort of thing. She's got her recruits telling them they will have somewhere to live . . ."

Barry snorted quietly.

"And their dream jobs."

"Which we both know will be nightmare jobs."

"Yes, and they'll be exchanging this prison for another far worse. Ashley and I have spoken to a couple of people, gotten them to reconsider, but it's far too big a task in the short time we have."

"Do you have names for Jacquelyn's agents?"

"Jerilyn and Clare," I replied. "They're the only names we've been told so far."

"Hmm. We know Jacquelyn is nearby. She's been seen."

A shudder went through me. "Barry, I don't know how to stop this, and we've promised the women a way out of here. We're not leaving our friends in a place run by her."

"Hmm," Barry repeated. "That will be down to you and Ashley as field agents, I'm afraid."

"Agreed, but we need a bit more time."

"Got any ideas?"

I grinned. "Indeed I do," I replied, and then I told him my plan.

Nine p.m. came and went. The women were counted in the dorms, and everybody began to quiet down for the evening. The lights were turned out, and the fans drowned out any ancillary noises. I kept checking my watch, but time was moving at a snail's pace: 9:15 p.m., 9:23 p.m., 9:29 p.m.—and then, the shriek was deafening.

The fire alarms began to go off, one by one. The squawking caught everyone off guard. Every woman in my dorm sat up in her bed and looked around. Nobody seemed to know what was happening, but nobody moved. That was the thing about this environment—you learned quickly not to trust or believe in anything or anyone, so even when something happened like a life-threatening emergency, such as a tornado warning or a fire alarm, nobody moved—they waited and watched until someone moved first—at which point everyone would follow.

The prison was in chaos. The guards came running from all over, including—to my immense satisfaction—Ms. Jerilyn and Ms. Clare. We were all evacuated immediately to the gymnasium, women joining us from every direction as we ran through the halls. Everyone was put into dorm lines, and then the count began.

We sat . . . and sat . . . and sat, but that didn't matter. My plan had turned out to be as effective as it was simple. By the time we'd been given the all clear to return to our dormitories early in the hours of Saturday morning, every single woman in prison, both guard and inmate, had been accounted for. Our tech genius Deacon Barry had made right on his promise to tamper with the alarms. We had foiled Jacquelyn's plans.

At least for now.

Back in our beds, finally. Everyone exhausted, and I was feeling empowered. I finally felt like we were on track to complete this mission and get out of here—somehow. I stared up at the darkness, noticing how extremely quiet this room was at this moment with all these people in it asleep.

BAM!

Everybody in the dorm leaped out of their beds and hit the floor. What was that? I instinctively looked out the window, expecting a thunderstorm, but there was no inclement weather to speak of.

"Oh my gosh, was that a bomb?"

"What do we do?"

Ms. Washington came running into the dorm. "Everybody with me now!"

"What's going on?"

"It appears that there was an explosion, and the center of the building has been destroyed. We need to make sure everybody is safe, and then we will figure this out."

"Hey, did you hear that?"

"Are we being bombed or something?"

"Aw, c'mon, it's Saturday! What about my sleep in?" That was from Pauline, who was always the most reluctant to get out of bed.

"I need a shower. Can't we just take a shower?"

Everyone was talking on top of everyone else. We were feeling no sense of danger or attack.

"Okay, everybody, just follow me. We had a gas pipe burst, and it exploded into the administrative hallway, but nobody was hurt. The fire department is on the way, along with the gas company. Come on—we need to get you out of here, just in case."

Still dressed in our pajamas, we filed silently out of our dorm behind Ms. Washington. The air sirens were going off, and women were spread out across the field—a field of bodies. I blinked and realized I had been mistaken. Some were lounging, some were reading books, some were just talking. The sun was up, and the bright, cloudless blue sky gave me the shivers, setting my mind back to many years ago and the incidents of 9/11.

As I walked out through the fence to join them, I heard more sirens approaching from the distance. *Are they for us?* I wondered, but mostly I paid them no attention, for that was what I had learned to do after being here for so many months, and my training with HGS had programmed me not to have anything to do with the authorities.

Sometimes we had no choice but to cooperate with law enforcement. After all, although we have superpowers, there are some things we can't do. We aren't a whole legal system unto ourselves; we're not capable of trying and jailing criminals. And in our last mission, we did end up turning people into the law so they could be tried. We still believed in justice, in theory, even if the system had many holes, in practice. Overall, though, the team knew that the police could not be trusted. Jacquelyn and the Paoluccis' influence ran deep into the heart of the powers that be, in virtually every jurisdiction where their syndicate operated, corrupting everyone from ordinary beat cops to prosecutors to judges. For all we knew, even the courthouse stenographers were probably taking kickbacks!

Hours later, a guard's voice resounded through a bullhorn— "Everybody back for the count!"—and the flock of women quickly lined up by the gate.

"What's going on?"

"Seems there is a threat . . . not sure . . . just have to have everybody back to their dorms for safety," Ms. Washington said quickly, referring to her clipboard. "Okay, Dorm One, head out."

We trooped back to our bunks, feeling deflated. There was no TV, no electricity, no water—we couldn't even go for a shower before we changed out of our pajamas and pulled on our jumpsuits. The dorm was stagnant— no fans running, and no air moving. Ugh!

"There has been a threat, and we are on lockdown until further notice," Ms. Washington advised us. "Just do the best you can."

Do the best we can? I had never been so happy to have a transistor radio. I pulled it out, glad that I had remembered to replace the batteries last week and dialed in to a local radio station where the regional baseball game was being broadcast. Settling back into my bunk, I resigned myself to a sweaty afternoon and lost myself in the commentary.

"Hey, Kathryn?" Ashley was poking me, but I was in such a daze, I hadn't even noticed.

"Yeah, what's up?"

"Come with me."

I switched off my radio, laid it on my pillow, and jumped down off the top bunk and followed her around the corner to the door of our porch area. Most of the women were sitting out there with the door propped open. The humid air was better than no air at all.

Following Ashley into the field beyond our dorm, I looked where her pointing finger indicated a small cutout on the porch's base. I had never noticed it before.

"We have to go down there," she whispered.

"What? Is that safe? How do you even know about it?"

"I went to confession." Ashley grinned. "Come on."

I tried to stop her, but she lifted the latch and pulled me down with her before anybody noticed. The darkness engulfed me, and it took a few moments before my eyes adjusted.

"Ashley, what are we . . ."

"Shh!"

We climbed down a ladder, our feet feeling their way in the darkness, and followed a low tunnel as it curved around a bend. There, the tunnel got broader and taller, and I felt a whoosh of fresh air breeze past. As my eyes became more accustomed to the gloom, I noticed the tilework along the walls was all intact. Had someone been using these tunnels recently, maintaining them?

"Hey—how you guys doing?" Greg's voice rang out from the other end of the dark hallway.

"What are you doing here? We're gonna be in huge trouble! They'll think Ashley and I escaped, and then who knows what will happen to us? This is unacceptable. Somebody tells me what's going on!" My voice was high-strung.

"Kate, chill! While you and Ashley have been inside, we have been tracking Jacquelyn. She's getting rich off these private prisons, thanks to lavish government contracts—which of course she secures through bribery and other kinds of kickbacks. Then, she gets richer from exploiting the prisoners' labor. But that's not all. We've found out exactly why she's interested in the prison system: under cover of reform, she's smuggling out women to use for drug trafficking. They're the lucky ones—others are trafficked themselves, sold into slavery and prostitution, and that's not just the women—she's doing the same in the men's prisons. There's a men's facility just up the road from here, and these tunnels link the two. Just up there," he pointed to a passageway leading off to the left, rising sharply— "leads to your commons field, and this one"—he indicated a similar tunnel— "connects with your gymnasium. She promises them freedom, telling them they've been specially selected. Only they were selected long before they were locked away—selected to be falsely accused of crimes they never committed so Jacquelyn can have an unlimited supply of slave labor."

Greg shuddered, and then continued.

"She gets them out through these tunnels and ships them off to God knows where and brutally uses them until they die. Their families never know what happened to their loved ones, and the system is so much under Jacquelyn's influence that even the good people in power don't dare question or try and figure it out for fear they'll be the next to disappear."

"But if she owns the prisons," I asked, "why doesn't she just take the recruits out through the front door?"

"She doesn't want to make her actions public," replied Greg. "You can imagine the interest the media would take if streams of prisoners started walking out the door at the prison owner's request. The public doesn't know you've been falsely accused; to them, you deserve all you get."

Ashley and I looked at each other. "Good to know," Ashley grumbled sarcastically.

"That's why, I believe, she gets her agents to tell the recruits to keep things quiet," Greg said.

Ashley and I exchanged glances again. Good job our cellmates were so rubbish at keeping a secret.

"The next group of women was supposed to leave here last week, but you and Barry managed to foil that and buy us some time, Kate. Good thinking, but the next run is just before ten tonight. We need your help. We need to stop this once and for all."

"What about on the men's side? Who's going to stop that?"

"That'll be me." Michael's voice took me by surprise as he emerged from the shadows of one of the other tunnels leading off from the space, we were in. "Chief rule breaker at your service. I've been inside on a false charge for over six months."

"Whoa, you too?" I said, shaking my head.

"Yeah, but it's cool. I've made friends . . . and probably enemies, but I can't do a lot about that. We're out of here tonight."

"How did Jacquelyn know where we were?"

"Do you think Raphael would recruit a rotten apple, Ashley?" I said. "My best guess is that we were meant to end up in jail."

"But we all knew at the beginning that it would be a setup. I just didn't see it happening this way."

"With a mission, yes."

"Woo!" said Michael. "That Raphael. He's got one crazy sense of humor."

"Look, we need to get back before we're missed. So, Greg, what's the big plan?"

"The locks work off a central system in both prisons," replied Greg. "It's a simple enough procedure to ensure the doors to the porches don't lock tonight. Oh, and the cameras covering that area will have a temporary malfunction too. This will allow you and Ashley to get down here and join us."

"We'll be bringing some friends," Ashley said.

"Ashley's right. We've bonded with a lot of people in there, and we promised to get them out," I added.

"Me too," said Michael. "Including a friend of yours, Kate."

"Huh? Who?" I asked but received only an enigmatic smile in return.

"That's all cool," said Greg. "Your friends wouldn't be safe if we left them inside, so the more, the merrier. Then it's over to Raphael and Musa to work their magic and make sure they're safe. So, the plan for tonight: there is a tunnel about twenty feet from here that joins the one I pointed out to you girls earlier—it goes underneath the gymnasium. That's where Jacquelyn's agents are going to smuggle out the women."

"What happens if we encounter Jacquelyn?" I asked.

"Well, you can't kill a shapeshifter with a gun or knife. The only way to kill them, according to Raphael, is to have someone with healing abilities 'melt' into them by touching them. Once the melding of bodies begins, the shapeshifter can't escape and will eventually dissolve into nothing. But it takes time, and the process must be completed, or she will survive." He looked at me meaningfully. "So, Kate, it's got to be you. Ashley will help get the other women to get away, but you have to be the one to touch Jacquelyn and destroy her." Michael gave me a look that was part fear and part panic. In that moment, I felt as if the entire weight of this mission had been put onto my shoulders.

My thoughts flashed back to when I had laid my hand on Jacquelyn's arm at the royal party in Finland, and she had melted—literally—to the floor. However, she didn't die; she just shifted away. Why didn't she die then? What made this time different? Was it because I somehow had not seen the "process" through to its completion?

"She's my aunt. Can I be responsible for killing my aunt, no matter how awful I think she is, and how will I know when it's done?" I asked.

"Kate, this is the only way to stop her. You are the only one with the healing power. Apparently, that gift also has an inverse: the capacity to kill a shapeshifter."

I wasn't at all happy about the plans for my night's work. "When we stop her, then what?"

"Honestly, I have no idea," Greg said.

"Okay, listen, we have to get back. We'll see you guys tonight."

"Sure thing." Greg offered an encouraging smile. "We'll be waiting right here."

"Okay, it's a date," Ashley tossed her hair back and smiled at Greg. Then she and I scrambled back up the hanging stairs and quietly lifted the hatch.

"Where have you guys been?" asked Wanda, peering over the side of the porch as we emerged from the opening underneath her.

And so it begins.

CHAPTER TEN

The rest of the afternoon dragged on. It was only a few hours we had to wait, but it seemed like days. The women we'd talked into coming with us—the ones we trusted—were buzzing with excitement, and I could see them almost bursting at the seams as they tried to contain it. Every time I looked up, I caught the eye of at least one of my friends and got a conspiratorial grin in response—so much for acting naturally, as Ashley and I had warned we had to do.

So as not to make things worse, I sat in my bunk and buried my head in a book, pretending to read as I thought about what I had heard from Greg. The surprise was that all this time, Michael had been going through the same thing as Ashley and me, only in the men's prison. I thought about what was coming and the role I had to play in it.

This job never failed to surprise me.

Luckily, when Ashley and I had emerged from the tunnel after our meeting with Greg and Michael, the only women on the porch had been the ones who we intended to take out with us. Well, it wasn't that surprising, really—Christina, Wanda, Caprice, Ashley, and I had become a tight-knit group over the months we'd been inside, and Krystal had slotted in just fine. I was glad I hadn't allowed myself to be swayed by the silly name, or the tears when she had arrived—Krystal had turned out to be one of the strongest and most loyal women I knew in prison, and I had no doubt she was worth saving. I was shocked that Pauline wasn't there too, but she was nowhere to be seen. I couldn't even find her in the gym, which was where she spent most of her time. Sad though it was, it seemed there was nothing I could do to get her out of here.

The power and water had come back on while we'd been gone, so a lot of the other women were out of the dorm, some enjoying showers, others catching up on their Saturday TV fix. Ashley and I took advantage of the opportunity to shower and freshen up in preparation for our adventure later, once we'd filled in the women on the porch on a simplified version of tonight's plans. Okay, we'd probably pick up some dirt down in those tunnels, but I hadn't wanted to start out smelling worse than a skunk. A shower had helped pass some time.

Finally, the words I had been waiting to hear: "Lights out—goodnight, ladies."

Bless you, Ms. Washington. I'm going to miss your cheerful face, but I'm not going to miss this place, no siree. Not one bit.

A hush fell over the dorm. I sat up and tried to get Ashley's attention, but it was hard—she was across the room, and in the dark, shadow puppets were the best I could do. The televisions were still blaring in the living room. Because it was Saturday, the TVs would be on for another hour, and luckily for us, a lot of the girls in our dorm were huge *American Idol* fans, so most of them were still up and chatting in the living room area. I could hear them arguing about who should win *Idol*.

I had packed my journal and gotten dressed, so I was ready to go. I headed toward the back door, and Ashley joined me a few seconds later.

"I am terrified about this," she whispered.

"Don't be," Caprice was suddenly right behind us, and her voice startled me.

"Yeah, but I don't want to get caught. I just want to go home."

"Me too, Ash. It's cool. You said it was cool."

"So, we're not backing down now," added Wanda.

"Yeah, c'mon, Ash, you were so sure earlier." That was from Christina.

"You're right." Ashley quietly moved the plant away from the hatch without saying any more, unlatched it, and down we went. I went last, carefully closing the hatch behind me, feeling absurdly satisfied when I heard the catch click into place.

C'mon, Kathryn. We've barely started, and you're getting excited about closing a door?

By the time I caught up with the others, Greg was already handing out flashlights. Barry was distributing clothes to our friends behind him, laughing his infectious laugh as Christina insisted on continuing to call him Deacon Jerry.

"There's plenty to go around. The guys' clothes are in that bag over there if Michael ever gets here."

"Guys?" asked Wanda, looking up from lacing a new pair of sneakers. "Who's Michael?"

"Oops, forgot to tell you that bit." I remembered what had slipped my mind just seconds earlier. "Michael's our colleague. We only found out today he's been in the men's prison over the road almost as long as we've been in here."

"Why? What did he do wrong?"

"Same as us. Nothing."

As I turned, I noticed who was standing behind Barry, smiling at me.

"Scott! Oh my goodness, Scott!" I ran into his arms and held on to him as if I'd never let go.

"Get a room, you guys!" Michael's familiar voice reached us a second before he emerged from the tunnel behind us and clasped his arms around our shoulders. "Good to see you again, Scott."

In that moment, I felt alive. Time stopped for me, and for one brief second, I was in a life where none of this had happened and we were all together, things were normal, we were happy, we were safe. In that moment, there was solidarity.

"Uh, hello?" I said, turning to Michael and pulling a face.

"Yeah, good to see you too, Kate, but we did only just meet, like, a few hours ago. I haven't seen this dude in over a year."

A group of six or seven men had followed Michael through the tunnels and into a cavernous opening, hollowed out and echoing every little sound; it was difficult to count them precisely as a group of people milled around, sorting out clothing, then melting into the shadows to get changed in private. That was, all except Caprice, who stripped down to her bra and panties in full view and nearly made Michael's eyes pop out of his head. With a grin, she treated him to a cheeky shake of her shapely butt before pulling on a pair of jeans.

"So, Michael," I said, not worrying too much about keeping my voice down. We knew Jacquelyn's plans were due to be put into action shortly before the TVs went off at ten, so we still had a good half hour to go. "Who's this friend of mine?"

"Uh yeah, where's he gone? Tom? Tom, over here."

A figure sprawled out from the shadows, dressed in straight blue jeans and a Nike T-shirt, his shoulders hunched and his head down. Then he raised his head and looked me straight in the eye.

With that, I came face-to-face with my former neighbor, Tom Morgan. My betrayer.

"He's no friend of mine," I growled when I finally found my voice.

"Not the time or the place to discuss it," said Ashley. "We need to get these guys and gals out of here before Jacquelyn turns up."

"Who's—" Krystal began, but Ashley hushed her.

"No time now. We'll see you again, and we'll fill you all in then."

"You FBI?" asked Wanda. I laughed, remembering when I'd asked Raphael that same question.

"No," I replied. "It's way weirder than that. Go with Scott and Barry."

"Barry?"

"Deacon Jerry. They'll get you out to a safe house."

"But what then?" asked Wanda desperately. "I got a husband, two kids—all I want to do is hold them in my arms, but as soon as I show up at home, surely I'll just be arrested again."

"You'll be fine," Ashley purred, her persuasive powers coming to the fore again. "Our boss—well, he can fix things."

"He's a fixer?"

"He rights wrongs."

"Sounds like an angel," said Christina, her precious rosary as ever in her hands.

You don't know how right you are.

CHAPTER ELEVEN

All was quiet once the men and women who had broken out with Ashley, Michael, and I disappeared behind Scott and Barry. For the first time in over a year, it was just the team—my team—together on a mission again. I could see the whites of their eyes gleaming in the gloom, the occasional flash of teeth in a grin suggesting the others were as happy to be back on the chase as I was. This was what we did. This was what we had been born to do.

Silence, the smell of mold from the old tunnel, and suddenly a fresh breeze. Someone had opened a hatch on the outside. Was it Barry, Scott, and the others leaving? Or was it someone entering the tunnel?

Ashley looked at me, indicating she could hear the conversation. Within moments, the rest of us could too.

"Shush! We don't want anybody to hear us."

"Who is going to hear us? We are down here alone, almost to freedom."

"I can't believe this is happening, and I am so excited to be free."

I could identify a couple of voices, but there were many that I didn't know. Ashley gestured to Greg and Michael, indicating that she could hear other people approaching from the direction of the men's prison, and they crept off into a tunnel on the opposite side of the cavern.

No matter which way we walked, the tunnels all seemed to look and smell the same. The walls had been dug out decades ago, and the beams that supported the dirt were naturally wearing away. The dust mixed with earthy and metallics was a musty mixture akin to aged garlic. And it was silent, very silent.

Greg had ditched his regular clothes and was now clad in gray prison-issue clothing like the rest of us. Ashley and I snuck into the tunnel on our side and waited where it converged with the passageway from the gymnasium, where the murmur of voices was getting louder.

That was when we heard the man.

"Okay, listen up." He spoke in a stern voice; commanding, threatening. It was not the kind of voice that put you at ease. Jacquelyn must have found a replacement for Turner. "My name is Johnny Sanchez, and here's how this is going to happen—you are going to go to the exit tunnel, where cars are waiting. Once you crawl out of the tunnel, someone will hand you fresh clothes. Take off your prison-issue clothes right then and there, and put on the fresh ones, then head to the car, okay?"

"When do we get to meet Ms. Raven?" one of the women asked. Ashley and I looked at each other in the gloom, and I saw the white gleam of her teeth as she grinned.

Ms. Raven? I remembered the way large blackbirds had plagued my life since childhood and shuddered.

"Meet her? Meet her?" Sanchez's voice was getting louder with a tinge of annoyance. "She is always around. At some point, you will all meet her, but for now, know she is watching. So, do what I say."

"Hey, what was that explosion all about earlier? They said it was some kind of threat." The talkative woman wasn't going to go down without a fight.

"Oh, that." Sanchez, with his oversized belly and oily mustache, gave a chuckle that didn't hold an ounce of good humor. "Just a little diversion to make sure all the attention was elsewhere. Apart from these good ladies here." I heard a giggle that sounded suspiciously like it came from Ms. Clare. "We didn't want any silly fire alarms malfunctioning again and ruining our plans, now did we? Keep moving and shut up."

The tunnels seemed to go on endlessly when all at once you would come upon a convergence. It was as if someone walked straight for miles, then randomly decided to turn. We could see sections of the wall worn away, and other signs that maybe these convergence points were entry points that had been filled in from above.

As we reached the two tunnels' convergence, I was dismayed to see Pauline among Jacquelyn's recruits, but that was the moment I knew exactly what I had to do. As she passed me, I reached out from my shadowy alcove and tugged at her sleeve. She turned and squinted into the shadows.

"Kathryn, what are you?"

"Shh! I need to get in front of you, okay?"

"Okay."

I jumped into the line in front of Pauline, crawled up to the trap door, and was lifted out by a burly man with bushy eyebrows.

Fresh air.

It seemed to me that the air smelled differently. I believe after all of those months incarcerated that I had forgotten how fresh the air could actually be when you weren't surrounded by walls and barbed wire. I gulped it in.

"Here—change. Over there," he commanded brusquely in a thick Polish accent. Jeans, a sweater, and tennis shoes were thrust in my direction, and I followed the line of women toward the waiting cars. It was then I noticed the driver in the lead car was Scott. He looked at me and nodded. I put my head down, kept walking.

"Sanchez, are we done yet?" A woman's voice, harsh and cold, shot through the silent night. Jacquelyn. She was here. But where? I looked around but couldn't see anything in the darkness.

"Yes, ma'am, almost done."

"Get a move on it, this shouldn't be taking so long." A figure emerged from the gloom, striding over the uneven ground on a precarious pair of killer Jimmy Choo heels as quickly as if she were wearing sneakers. As she passed me, I hunched into my clothes, hoping against hope she wouldn't sense my presence. She didn't. She appeared to be on a mission of her own.

"You!" she snapped. "We need to cut your hair."

I turned to see whose hair needed cutting and was relieved and horrified in equal measures to see Ashley—relieved that she had followed my lead, horrified to see the woman of my nightmares, Jacquelyn, was gripping a bunch of her hair in her fist.

"I like my hair." Ashley's voice quivered.

"It's not what we need. It's not what they pay for. Change and go to the first car."

"I will not cut my hair, and you can't make me!" Ashley yelled, twisting out of Jacquelyn's grip, and delivering a thump to her stomach. Jacquelyn barely even flinched.

"You will do what I say—I own you now. Do you want me to call in your 'escape'?"

"You can't. You aren't in charge of me—and I know who you are, Jacquelyn!"

Jacquelyn's mouth gaped, and her skin paled as recognition dawned on her features. "You!"

Ashley's face twisted into a sneer. "Yes, me, and you are not taking these women."

"This stops now!" While watching the confrontation between Ashley and Jacquelyn, I hadn't noticed that Michael had snuck up behind them. Out of the corner of my eye, I saw Greg ushering a line of people in prison-issue clothing toward SUVs parked on the men's prison side of the road.

The men's prison and the women's prison are down the road from each other, but as we followed the tunnels, we discovered they were actually only a few miles apart. They had been purposefully built in the form of pentagons to confuse those going inside so that there would be no thought of escape. It would be like to trying to figure out a Rubik's cube if all the sides were the same color – how do you really know which is the right way? *Interesting design choice*, I thought.

Meanwhile Jacquelyn's henchmen, who had been escorting them, rushed over in a bid to protect her. Musa emerged from the driver's seat of the lead vehicle on the men's side and gave me a thumbs-up, and I allowed myself a quick grin.

It looked like the team on the outside did a good job of infiltrating the transport Jacquelyn's had lined up for her latest recruits.

Then, I was back in focus. While everyone was distracted by the confrontation between Ashley and Jacquelyn, I inched my way backward to find myself squarely beside her.

It was now or never.

CHAPTER TWELVE

"It's over," I said, grabbing Jacquelyn by the arm.

"You!"

I smiled, victorious. "Me."

"Just like your father . . ." Her voice drifted off as she wriggled, trying to release herself from my sturdy grip. "Let go of me!" she cried with a high-pitched snap. "Sanchez!"

Like an obedient dog, the swarthy man came running immediately.

"Stay away!" Michael challenged Sanchez.

Sanchez went to brush him out of the way, but Michael grabbed hold of his arm, pulling him off balance. Trying to twist his way out of Michael's grip, Sanchez turned to him, snarling, and Michael wound a leg around Sanchez. Taking Sanchez's feet out from under him, Michael dropped to the ground with him, trying to overpower him. Michael was strong, but Sanchez, it appeared, was just as powerful. I had no doubt it was a good wrestling contest, but I wasn't able to stand and watch.

The air was thick with the smell of must, a cloudless night showcasing the shadows the moon was casting across the fields, hills, and trees. I was vaguely aware of the roar of engines as the convoy of SUVs moved into position between Jacquelyn's henchmen and us, but my focus was on my hand as it melded right into her arm.

"It can't end this way," she said, looking at me. Right at me, almost as if she could see through me. As if she could read my thoughts, my fears.

"It has to end. This has gone on long enough."

She yanked free of my grip. This would be harder than I expected. She wasn't going to go down without a fight. Suddenly, her voice shifted into the sweetest, old familiar tone. She looked at me, smiling, and her entire face seemed to soften. Was this real or was she purposely shifting to be this way in my sight?

"Oh, Cinnamon," the voice was deep, calm, and protective, but where was it coming from? "You are my Snoop . . . always know your purpose and you will be just fine in this world." The voice, it was my dad. I turned and looked directly at Jacquelyn.

"That's right," she said with a grimace. The voice had come out of her. "How can you do this to me, Kathryn? You know we're related."

"My dad, I just . . . how did you . . .?" I stammered, trying to regain my ground.

"I can do so many more things than you could ever imagine, and so could you if you would just open up your eyes and realize it," she said coldly.

I wanted to destroy her. I *needed* to destroy her. But was this against moral code? After all, she was my aunt by blood. I knew we had to stop her and the organization that she was running, but my plan had never been to *destroy* her.

I was not willing to wait on others making decisions; rather, I was moving forward, standing in my own power. And this needed to be done.

"After all, I am your Auntie Jacquelyn," she said, her voice taking on a wheedling quality. Had she just read my thoughts? "I can hear what you are thinking, I know what you are doing, I am stronger than you think you are–and stronger than your father ever was."

To kill her would mean killing off a part of me, a familial lineage that I knew had always been there but tried hard not to acknowledge. Would this change my powers? Would this change my personality? At this point, it didn't matter; I needed to do this for myself, for the team, for the world.

I lunged towards Jacquelyn, grabbing her arm and twisting hard. Caught off guard, she teetered on her heels as she tried to unlatch herself from me. This time, the nexus was too powerful for her to overcome. Smoke oozed out of her head and neck, reminding me of a car that wouldn't start even as you rev the engine over and over. She was trying to shapeshift and get away, but something was stopping her.

It was me. I was stopping her.

The zing shot through me like a bolt of electricity. I am quite sure she felt it too. The warmth built up quickly, and I recalled the feeling from healing in the past—except this time, it was different. Instead of healing Jacquelyn, I was melting her—literally.

Then her words echoed through my mind. *How can you do this to me? I'm your father's sister . . . father's sister . . . father's sister . . ."*

Abruptly, I let go of her arm, and Jacquelyn slumped to the ground, unmoving.

The crunch and squeal of tires sounded as the SUV came to within a foot of where I was standing, and Greg flung himself out and dashed towards me "What did you do?"

I just stared at him, words escaping me. What had Jacquelyn just said to me? How did she put words in my head?

Greg was speaking to me. "Did you kill her?"

Her body had been there a moment ago, lifeless. Now all I saw was a pile of burnt bones, singed around the edges.

I stared. No words. All around me, the women who had come out of the prison with Sanchez were evidently shocked, crying and hugging in confusion.

Pauline approached me. It looked like she was about to take hold of my arm, then clearly thought better of it and withdrew her hand.

"Kathryn, what just happened?" she asked.

"This woman is one of the evilest, um . . .people in this world. She's been using these facilities to recruit people for drug and sex trafficking. You were never going to be free."

"How do you know that?"

Ashley looked at her thoughtfully. "Just trust me," she said. I saw she had Ms. Jerilyn in an arm lock. "This one's coming with us. We want a word." Ms. Jerilyn just whimpered; all trace of the aggressive woman she'd been inside the jail having vanished. Of Sanchez and the rest of Jacquelyn's bullies, there was no sign.

"Excuse me if I'm being dumb," said Pauline, "but what woman?"

"Huh?"

"You said that Ms. Raven was the evilest person in the world or something. What woman do you mean?"

"Oh, yeah. You'd been told she's called Ms. Raven. She's Jacquelyn."

"So, where is she? I'd like to get a look at the shrew who was going to sell me into God knows what."

"Her bones are lying right there."

I turned to look—and groaned. There was nothing but a patch of singed grass where Jacquelyn's bones had been. Jacquelyn was a master at disappearing right from under our noses.

"I need some water," I said.

"Here," Ashley said, handing me a chilled bottle. I chugged down at least half without stopping for breath, then promptly vomited it back up onto the ground where I had left Jacquelyn for dead.

Focus, Bek! I scolded myself. I could never bring myself to think of my name as Paolucci, so I kept using my mother's maiden name. The name I'd grown up with after my evil aunt made sure my father lost first the love of his family, and then the ultimate sacrifice—his life. *She's gone. Somehow, she's gone. Get over it.*

"We need to do whatever we can to get these people back home," I said, my voice strangely hoarse.

"Agreed."

Pulling myself back into the present, I climbed into the tail SUV, driven by a woman I recognized as one of Raphael's tech geniuses—a kind of female Barry. In between Ashley and me in the backseat was a handcuffed Ms. Jerilyn.

"Where are we headed?" I asked.

"Raphael has a plane waiting for us—we are going home," replied Ashley. "Good-bye, Alaska."

"What about the others left inside the prison?"

"Tomorrow, there will be a notification from the governor's office, shutting down that facility," said our driver, who had introduced herself as Rose. "With the help of some sympathetic lawyers, we have gone through the records of all five hundred women who were in there, and of that group, only two showed legal cause to be incarcerated. Of the men, only four had committed a crime of any sort. The cases against them were thin as air—there was no evidence, and no procedural reason to keep everyone detained without trial or convicted on the flimsiest of grounds.

"We were also able to construct a paper trail documenting the cash the Paolucci family used to poison every courthouse, every prosecutor, every judge in the jurisdiction. Not to mention a lot of cops who were on the take, and officials who were bribed into privatizing the prison in the first place."

"There are a lot of people who are not going to be happy tomorrow, but that's their problem, not ours," said Ashley. "We are heading back home, and to our beds. For this one"—she nodded her head at Ms. Jerilyn— "a lot of awkward questions."

"What about the other women who got out with us and with her? And the guys?"

"Raphael has arranged for them all to be taken to a safe house until everything's done tomorrow, and they're officially pardoned," Ms. Jerilyn said. "Then they will be transported back to their homes, wherever they come from. Apart from that guy you don't like—Tom Morgan?"

"Morgan," I corrected. "He and his wife set me up. They were the reason I was in jail in the first place, saying I was dealing drugs."

"Drugs? You?"

"Yeah, crazy, right? And get this—they said I was using their kids as runners. Two little girls, ages thirteen and ten."

"I get why you don't like him."

Ms. Jerilyn chose that moment to start bleating. "I never wanted to be a part of it. It was all Clare's idea—you gotta believe me!"

"We don't," snapped Ashley. "Save your excuses for the people who are going to interrogate you. We're not interested."

I sat in the SUV, looking out the window as a child during their first car ride. I had forgotten the feeling of tires, the speed of the world whooshing by, and the ability to just observe. As I noticed the fields and treelined roadways pass by my window, out of the corner of my eye a flash of something dark and glossy almost hidden by the night sky. Squinting, I made out a solitary raven flying away. As I watched the bird ascend, my instinct kicked in, making me shudder as if I was stepping into a walk-in freezer.

It wasn't over.

The car silently drove up to the private plane, and Raphael was waiting for us. He greeted us with a broad smile as Ashley and I climbed out of the car.

"I hope you both realize how brave you are. What you did . . . well, it was beyond the scope of our normal missions. A triumph for society, not just HGS. We are hopeful this will be the spark needed to reform the whole justice system. Certainly Alaska is not the only place where corruption has taken root. But these things take time."

"So, what about the others?" Ashley asked. "Rose said they'd be cleared to go home tomorrow."

"That's my understanding. The agreement was that each of them will receive $500 and a plane ticket back to wherever they call home, allowing for a 'fresh start.' Their records will be expunged so these innocent victims can move forward with their lives. Same for the guys."

"What about me?" Ms. Jerilyn's plaintive wail carried from the back seat of the SUV.

Raphael bent down to investigate the car and address her. "Ah, Ms. Jerilyn, I wish I could say it was a pleasure. You have some questions to answer, so Rose here will be taking you to a holding facility. Please don't worry—you will be perfectly comfortable, and rest assured, we don't resort to bullying tactics."

Unlike you, Ms. J. The spiteful thought shot through my head, and I had to shake myself. That's not who I am.

To my relief, Tom would be flying to New York on a commercial airline, accompanied by Barry, so I wouldn't have to face him—yet. I wasn't sure why he was being brought to New York, though; his home was in Alaska, and I seemed to remember his mom lived in Miami. Oh well, that was a question for another day. For now, I was exhausted, I was dirty, and I was still dressed in my gray prison jumpsuit, having had no time to change clothes before everything had kicked off. Thankfully, we had the luxury of clean clothes and a shower on our private plane so that we could get comfortable.

As I stepped out of the shower, feeling relaxed and refreshed, Scott stood in front of me.

"I missed you," I said, feeling a huge smile spreading across my face.

"I missed you too."

"I didn't see you when I got on the plane."

"I was here the whole time."

"I can't imagine anything being harder than this mission."

"It impacted all of us deeply, in ways we didn't expect. It challenged me emotionally and not only as a husband. Seeing this flagrant abuse of your rights while not being able to do anything about it . . ." Scott shook his head. "I would have helped you if I could, but Raphael said that it was all part of the mission, and I had to stay away."

I smiled, feeling my chest warm with love for him. It wasn't so long ago that I wasn't sure if I wanted to stay with him. Scott had doubted my ability to lead this team and to be a part of something bigger than myself. Our long-distance relationship had taken a hit, and we were fighting often. Then, Scott stepped up in a big way. He asked me to marry him, joined the team, and supported me all the way.

"While you've been undercover, I have been looking over legal papers and doing odd administrative jobs for Raphael. The things he's had me reviewing are fascinating. There's more to Raphael than meets the eye."

You can say that again!

"Well, I'm glad he kept you busy." I smiled.

Done with talking for the moment, I grabbed Scott, kissed him on the cheek, and leaned back my seat to rest.

CHAPTER THIRTEEN

The brownstone was quieter than I remembered. Well, anything would be peaceful after spending so much time with so many women. Oh, to have my own space. What a luxury!

"Hey, are you getting situated?" Ashley asked, popping her head into the doorway of my room as I pulled on my clothes after a shower.

"Yep, it's slow, but I'm getting there."

"When will Scott be back?"

"Oh, probably tomorrow. He had to head to Chicago to check on some business. How about you? So, are you and Greg . . ."

"Debrief first," said Ashley, grinning. I grinned back.

"Okay, play it like that if you want, but the holding hands on the couch thing is a bit of a dead giveaway." I had caught them canoodling earlier that day on the living room couch. If they were trying to hide it, they were doing a lousy job at it.

Ashley skipped out of my room with a giggle. I didn't think I'd ever seen her so happy.

"Debrief at nine, debrief at nine, with coffee and cake, coffee and cake," she trilled as she ran down the stairs.

True to his word, Raphael had indeed supplied coffee and cake for our post-mission debrief. Walking into the conference room with Greg, Ashley, and Michael, I was as cheered by the array of sweet treats spread out across the table as I was by the comfortable familiarity of being back in the HGS offices. What I wasn't so cheered by was the sight of Tom Morgan, sitting beside Raphael on the other side of the table.

My entire body shook. It was as if an adrenaline-charged rage had been let loose within my veins. My face turned bright red.

Tom Morgan. Tall, lanky, and pale. For such a tall man, his arms were disproportionately short, which made him look almost comedic. I didn't know what to make of him. He was wearing a baseball cap, and a sweatshirt that said BOILERMAKERS. His jeans were old, the kind you might purchase when you are twenty-five and keep around because they became a favorite pair, but anyone looking at him could tell that those jeans had many years of wear on them. He looked nervous.

He should look nervous, I thought. *Maybe he thinks I'm going to haul off and punch him or something.*

Before I had a chance to direct any more than a glare in Tom's direction, Raphael leaped to his feet and greeted us all effusively.

"Welcome back, welcome back!" he gushed. "Please, help yourself to cakes. Let me pour you drinks. What's it to be? Tea? Coffee? Hot chocolate?"

The aroma of freshly brewed coffee was tempting, but feeling decadent, and that I'd earned it, I opted for hot chocolate, topped with whipped cream and marshmallows. Settling myself down opposite Tom, I sipped at my drink when Raphael handed it to me and closed my eyes in bliss.

"Um, Kate." Michael sat down beside me and nudged my arm. "Mustache."

"Huh?" I opened my eyes and looked at him. Picking up a napkin from the tables, he wiped a line of cream from my top lip, then tucked into the massive slab of lemon drizzle cake that had been sitting on the plate in front of him.

"Everyone served?" asked Raphael, scanning the table and rubbing his hands together. "Then let us begin. I'm sure you're all wondering what this gentleman is doing here today." Standing beside Tom, Raphael laid a hand on his shoulder. "Let me introduce you to Thomas Morgan of Onarde, Alaska. I believe Thomas is known to at least one of you—"

"As the schmuck who set me up, yeah," I interrupted, ten months' worth of frustration pouring out.

"Kathryn, I understand your anger," said Raphael, standing beside the chair where Tom sat. "However, there are things you don't know."

"Yeah right. Like I don't know how much she paid you," I bellowed as I pounded the table with my fists and rose to my feet. "A lot, judging by that fat Rolex you used to wear and the amount of Botox your wife had pumped into her face! What happened to dear Jessica, anyway?"

"I don't know," Tom cried, his voice hoarse. "After you were . . . you know . . ."

"After I was arrested? After I was carted off by the cops, accused of being a drug dealer and child abuser? After that, huh?"

"Look, Kathryn, I'm sorry. I am so, so sorry."

"Not good enough!"

"Hey, Kate," Greg interjected, "how about we listen to what the man has to say? If Raphael thinks it's important that he's here, then it's important, right?"

Of course, he was right, but I was still angry. Tight-lipped, I sat down again and leaned back, fixing Tom with an icy stare. He avoided my gaze and looked down at his hands that were twisting on the table in front of him. The fat Rolex was gone from his wrist. No doubt, one of Jacquelyn's agents in the men's prison had taken that away as a nice little bonus.

I felt an unworthy satisfaction at the thought.

"I don't know where Jessica is. By the time you were arrested, Kathryn, I was beginning to think something was way too dodgy about the deal Ms. Raven had offered us."

"Jacquelyn," corrected Raphael.

"Right. Okay. Right, Jacquelyn turned up on our doorstep, like, a month or so before you arrived, Kathryn. She said she was from the FBI—had all the right credentials in the name of Janice Raven. It all checked out—we phoned our local police department to find out how to confirm her story, and they said they'd check it for us. Within half an hour, a couple of cops were on our stoop, all 'Yes, Ms. Raven' and 'No,

Ms. Raven.' They assured us she was exactly who she said she was. I didn't know then what I know now."

"Which is?" asked Ashley.

"That corruption runs deep in this country." My team and I exchanged meaningful glances. "It's seriously scary when you think about it."

"We do more than think about it," said Raphael. "My wonderful team across the table here is doing something about it. Go on."

"Right, so Ms. Raven turns up and offers us serious money. She says she and her team had received intel that a notorious criminal would be moving into the condo above ours. She said this woman was known to be a drug dealer, but the authorities had never been able to pin any of her crimes on her. She always had a watertight alibi."

Ashley howled with laughter. "She could've been describing herself!"

"She said the woman was called Kathryn Milligan."

"That was the alias you gave me," I interrupted, looking accusingly at Raphael. "So, how did she know a month before I did where I'd be living and what name I'd be using?"

Raphael smiled benignly, choosing not to answer my question. He didn't need to. I transferred my glower from Tom to Raphael, who didn't seem fazed in the slightest.

"If we could let Thomas continue without interruption," he said, "we have a lot to get through today."

The team and I groaned. "A lot to get through," generally meant a journey—a long one, and we'd only just got back home from the most challenging trip of our lives.

"I know you've only just got back from a difficult mission," said Raphael—I'd long since stopped being surprised at his ability to read my thoughts— "but this can't wait, I'm afraid. Thomas, please continue."

Tom pulled himself up a little straighter at Raphael's support and finally managed to make eye contact with me. "She was amazingly persuasive. She offered us $500,000 upfront."

"Yeah, I would imagine that would be persuasive," I spat.

"Kate, shh," hissed Ashley, and Tom went on.

"With another $500,000 to follow on completion of the mission. You're right, Kate . . ."

"Who said you could call me Kate?" I roared, thumping the table, and jumping to my feet again. Ashley hauled me back down to my seat.

"Will you shut up!" she snapped. "Raphael said this is urgent, so while you're throwing a tantrum, don't you think that maybe, just maybe, there's someone out there badly in need of our help?"

That did it. She was right. I shut up.

"So yeah, we took the cash, we bought the SUV, we bought the new kitchen and the designer clothes. We bought a fat Rolex. Yeah, sure, we sold out, and we paid a high price for it. When I met you, Kathryn," Tom said, emphasizing my full name, "I knew—I just knew you weren't what she'd said you were. Remember I said I'd trust you with my life? I meant it, but it was like Ms. Ra—Jacquelyn anticipated that. The next time she came round, she had some big thug called Sanchez with her. He scared us witless, said we'd better not think about letting his boss lady down because he knew things about us. Things that could make life very uncomfortable for us. While you were living above us, Kathryn, he kept popping up where we least expected it—dropping the kids at school? He'd be there. Impromptu family day out? He'd be there. Then he decided it was time to hurry things along."

Tom lowered his head into his hands for a few seconds.

"Kathryn, in the end, we didn't betray you for money—we did it to save our kids. Sanchez started turning up in our condo. We'd go to kiss the girls goodnight, and he'd be in one of their rooms. In a kid's bedroom, for heaven's sake, sitting on the bed or lurking in the shadows. The girls were petrified of him, and we were petrified of what he'd do to them."

Tom looked close to tears, and for the first time, my heart went out to him. I thought of his daughters: two more innocents caught up in Jacquelyn's evil web of deceit.

"So the time had come. It was Jessica who called it in. I know you thought she hated you, Kathryn, but she didn't. Okay, she may have been a little jealous, thought I was hitting on you, but mostly, she was terrified for our girls, just like I was."

I thought Jessica was more than a little jealous and more than a little swayed by the money on offer, but I bit my tongue this time.

"So, Jessica went to the cops with the trumped-up charges. She planted the drugs in your condo. Then you were arrested and taken away. Geez, I felt terrible about that, and then I realized just what we'd gotten ourselves into—we'd sided with the bad guys. Bad guys aren't known for keeping their promises.

"That night, after the girls were asleep, Jessica and I talked. I mean, talked. I told her I was taking the girls far away from the danger, so I packed a few things, told the girls to gather whatever was important to them, and we caught a flight the very next day down to Florida. My mom lives in Pinecrest, in the suburbs of Miami. The girls were a bit upset to be leaving us behind, especially as we couldn't reassure them when they'd be able to come back home, but they're sensible kids. Jessica wasn't too happy as she and my mom have never been friends, but the kids love their grandma, and she loves them. She's got a house in a safe neighborhood, great for children."

"How much does your mom know?"

"Only that we'd run into a bit of trouble, no details. She wanted us all to leave Alaska right away and come live with her, but of course, Jessica disagreed. It had always been her dream to build a life in Alaska, a bit of a move away from the modern world, and she wasn't about to give it up quickly.

"So anyway, while I was in Florida—geez, I feel bad about this—enjoying a few days with Mom, Jessica was summoned in to see Ms. R— Jacquelyn in a secret location. Sanchez would be coming to collect her; there was no option to say no. She promised me she wouldn't say a word about where I was, and I know she wouldn't. She may not like Mom, but she loves our daughters to the end of the universe and back. We were speaking on the phone when Sanchez arrived to pick her up . . ."

Tom's voice faltered, and he looked down at his feet again. I saw tears drop down to the floor before Raphael silently handed him a box of tissues.

"Thanks," said Tom nasally, wiping his tears and blowing his nose. "Sorry, guys. She said she'd call me directly when she got back. Only she never did. When I left the girls with Mom in Weston and went back home, the condo was all shut up, dark and silent. Jessica had gone. Vanished. No word from her since."

"I'm sorry," I whispered, and Tom looked at me in amazement. "No really, Tom, I am."

"Um, thanks." With another sniffle or two, Tom continued. "Of course, I went to the cops. Stupid, really—you'd think the warning bells that they'd vouched for Jacquelyn would have told me all I needed to know, but when you've been brought up to trust the cops, and anyone in authority, as I have, it's a hard habit to break. So, I went to the cops, and they laughed in my face and said Jessica had probably left me 'cause I'm a lowlife—I won't repeat what they called me—and then, they slapped handcuffs on me, removed all my possessions, and shipped me out to a holding facility. My crime? Drug dealing. Ironic, huh?"

I just smiled wryly.

"That was that until Saturday night happened, and now here we are."

"Here we are true," said Raphael. "Thank you, Thomas. I now throw this meeting open to the team. Is there anything you need to clarify? I believe we pretty much exchanged all the news we needed to exchange on the journey home."

"Sure thing," I said, glancing around at my team and seeing them nod their heads in agreement. "So, Tom, have you spoken to your mom or your kids since you got out?"

"Of course. The first thing I did was phone them, as soon as I could get to a phone, which was at the airport, before boarding my flight to New York. A bit noisy, but I had to hear their voices. The girls were a bit tearful, but they're fine, just fine. Mom, too, although she said there's still been no sign or word from Jessica."

"Uh-oh," said Michael, staring into the middle distance. I knew that look. My blood froze.

"A ripple?" I asked.

"Mm-hmm." Michael, and his clairvoyance, often surprising him—and by extension, us—with a glimpse of things happening simultaneously in our own universe.

"What did you see?"

"Clouds."

"Just clouds?"

"And a bad feeling. Scared. People are scared and confused. There's a smell, that distinctive smell."

This was new. Michael had never caught scents before.

"Smell of what?" I asked.

Michael turned to me, his face pale. "School."

"Um, Tom . . ." I cast my eyes over the table again. "I think you'd better call your mom again."

Wordlessly, Raphael handed Tom a cell phone, and we all sat silently as he switched it to speakerphone and dialed.

"Hello?" Tom's mom answered, sounding bright and cheerful, and we all breathed a sigh of relief.

"Mom, hi, it's Tom . . . um, I mean Thomas." Wincing, he whispered to us, "She hates when people shorten my name."

"Thomas, honey, good to hear from you. I tried the condo, but the answering machine picked up."

"Yeah, Mom, I'm in . . ." Tom broke off at a warning gesture from Raphael and amended what he'd been about to say. "I'm, um, not at home now. Are the kids around?"

There was a tinkle of laughter from the other end of the phone connection. "No, silly. They're in school. I thought it best to get them enrolled here—I didn't want to risk them missing out on their education."

Uh-oh. School.

"But it's a good thing you've called, dear. A friend of yours has dropped in to see me, thought he'd come by and share some iced tea with your old mom while he's vacationing in Miami. Yeah, nice guy." With a giggle, Mrs. Morgan lowered her voice. "Hot too. You know I like the Spanish guys, Thomas."

"Mom!"

"D'you wanna say hello? Hey, Johnny, come say hello to Tom."

"Hello, Tom," said a man's voice. It was vaguely familiar. Where had I heard that voice recently?

"It's your old pal, Johnny Sanchez."

CHAPTER FOURTEEN

Another day, the same airplane. There wasn't a moment to lose trying to find seats on a commercial airline; we'd all distinctly heard the cocking of Sanchez's gun over the phone, followed by Mrs. Morgan's terrifying whimper: "I don't think this guy is a friend of yours, is he, Thomas?"

Then the call had cut off.

With urgency, the name of the game—again—we'd all piled back onto Raphael's private jet and flown out of an airfield that was, as far as the general public was concerned, unused. An hour after the call had disconnected, we were airborne and heading south. Tom alternated between tense silence and beating himself up for not having warned his mom that there was a chance that Jacquelyn and her goons might turn up.

"She didn't know!" he wailed over the constant hum of the cabin's air flow. "If I'd told her about Sanchez . . ."

"Tom, stop this!" I commanded. "This isn't your fault. Your mom didn't . . ."

I stopped abruptly, aware that what I'd been about to say was hardly going to help the situation. Too late. Tom guessed, anyway.

"She didn't stand a chance against that violent creep. Yeah, I know. Heads, Mom loses; tails, she loses." Tom lapsed into another period of brooding silence.

We hadn't wanted Tom to come with us. This was the first time we'd set out on a mission with someone who wasn't part of the team in tow and having a "civilian" on board made me nervous. I could tell it made Ashley nervous too, and Michael was already in a heightened state of tension thanks to his glimpse through the time portal of the clouds and the school—whatever that was going to turn out to mean. Only Greg remained poker-faced; he always was the hardest one to read out of the team. Yes, we'd argued that Tom was more likely to be a liability than an asset, but he'd argued right back that he was not going to be staying in Manhattan. At the same time, his mom had a gun at her head in Miami, and his kids were in a school (which may or may not have had some ominous clouds descending over them) as we were standing around arguing. I'd turned to Raphael for support, but to my disbelief, Raphael sided with him.

I mentioned to Tom how his tagging along might hinder our chances of saving his mom and daughters.

"I think you might be surprised," Raphael said.

So, here we were, the team and Tom, flying to face heaven knew what in Florida.

The airplane touched down in Miami at five p.m.—luckily, New York and Miami are in the same time zone; my head was still messed up, adjusting from Alaskan time. Raphael had called ahead and arranged for a car to take us from the private airstrip—another deserted one—to the pleasant suburb where Tom's mom lived, and a sleek SUV was waiting for us, keys in the ignition, as we disembarked. Tom made for the driver's seat, but Ashley headed him off at the pass.

"No way, man," she said, sliding in behind the steering wheel and adjusting the seat to take her slight frame. "You're in no state to drive."

"What do you mean? We're in Florida."

"I mean," said Ashley, pushing him out of her way, "you're in no condition to drive!"

"But I know the area . . ." Tom argued, hanging on to the driver's door so Ashley couldn't close it. "I grew up here. You ever even been to Miami? You know where Pinecrest is?"

"Nope. Never been to Florida, but I have GPS."

Ashley started the engine as Greg, Michael, and I piled into the back seat. None of us wanted to sit next to a fidgeting and anxious Tom, so we wordlessly decided to leave the front passenger seat to him. "You are getting in, or what?"

"If anything happens to my mom while you're getting us lost in a place you've never been to before, I'll swing on you, so help me God. You and you and you and you." He pointed at each of us in turn. "And I don't care if some of you are women. My mom's life is on the line here, and you're . . ."

So Tom grumbled on and on. I'd tuned him out before we'd even left the airfield, focusing my mind for whatever the mission ahead of us might throw up, and I guess my team did the same thing. Tom's voice just became background noise, buzzing away until it was cut off abruptly as Ashley steered the SUV onto a broad avenue in Pinecrest, a pleasant suburb outside Miami. The silence from the front passenger seat startled us all, and we as one turned to look at Tom, who was gazing open-mouthed out of the windshield as Ashley pulled up at the side of the road.

"Your mom's place is off of this road, am I right?" she asked.

"Yeah, you're right. But how . . . but how?"

"As I said, trust me. Trust us. We got this." Ashley sounded a lot more confident than I felt. It was over four hours since we'd heard a violent and compassionless man cock a gun in Mrs. Morgan's house. I didn't want to dwell on what she'd been going through since then, how much terror—or worse— she'd been suffering. I just hoped she was still alive to feel terror—or worse.

"If you hang a left just up here," Tom was saying, "Mom's is the third house on the right. Big white-fronted place. You can't miss it. But you probably already know that, right?"

"Sure," said Ashley pleasantly. "Shall I blast the horn as we pull up, let Sanchez know we've arrived? No, Tom, we leave the car back here."

Turning the SUV around, Ashley pulled back onto the road we'd just left, drove for a quarter mile or so, and then found a space in the safe anonymity of a crowded parking lot.

"Is there a back way to your mom's?" I asked Tom as we all got out of the car. "The more overgrown, the better."

"We could cut across the neighbor's backyard," he replied, leading us at a brisk trot out of the parking lot and back toward his childhood home. "I was friends with their son, Peter, when we were kids. It's not overgrown as such, but Mark and Susan like to let it grow a little wild. Big on conservation, you know? It was a dream place to play back then."

"A dream place to sneak into your mom's property now, huh?"

"That's right. Mom said Susan and Mark are vacationing in Europe now, so no risk of them catching us prowling through their vegetation, no awkward questions. Come on!"

Tom turned left onto a narrow alleyway. Increasing his speed, he sprinted along, hardly breaking stride as he hauled himself into the branches of a mature Southern red oak tree and swung himself over a panel fence, disappearing into one of the yards that backed onto the alleyway.

"Yay! Tree climbing!" I cried gleefully at precisely the same moment Ashley complained, "Oh no, performing monkey time."

"I'll give you a leg up," I heard Greg offer Ashley as I pulled myself into the tree and over the fence. A moment later, her sweating, frowning face appeared over the wall and stared dubiously down at the vegetation beneath her.

"I gotta jump into that?" she asked.

"Sure," I said.

"Come on!" cried Tom, rocking on his heels, looking like he was going to take flight.

"Yeah, come on, Ashley," I urged, "before we lose Tom."

"Okay, I guess," she replied. Wrinkling her nose and closing her eyes, she swung her legs over the top of the fence and let herself drop into the yard as Greg appeared in the tree behind her. I pulled Ashley to her feet as he landed beside us.

"Where's Michael?" I asked.

"Gone," replied Greg. "He did that looking into a blank space thing, muttered something about solid clouds, and took off."

"You serious? He knows we're meant to stay together on missions."

"Well, we didn't do too badly for being separated in Alaska, did we? Don't forget, Mike was on his own in the men's prison."

"I guess, but how are we meant to find him?"

"We'll find him," said Ashley firmly. "Our more immediate problem is keeping up with Tom." I followed her sightline. There was no sign of Tom, but the dense brush around the impressive variety of trees in the backyard we'd dropped down into was trembling, indicating the direction he'd headed.

"Come on," I commanded. It felt so good to be retaking charge of my team, albeit one member light and with a stray civilian leading us into God knows what.

Truth be told, I hadn't felt much like a leader during this journey; however, maybe that was the point. Maybe it wasn't about what I did or how I did it, but who I was–did I carry the strength of a leader within me, no matter how tough things got? And did I exude it in the presence of others, so they could share that cool-headed confidence? I pondered this deeply and thought, *yes, so far, I have conducted myself like a leader.*

Without waiting to speculate, I dove into the shuddering shrubbery and followed Tom's trail, emerging at the edge of a well-tended lawn bordered by another panel fence.

"Over we go," I said, grinning sidelong at Ashley as I nodded toward a tree whose branches were still swaying from having borne Tom's weight.

"You don't say," she replied, taking a running jump, and grabbing hold of a sturdy branch, her toned arms lifting her slim body effortlessly up and over the fence.

"We'll make a performing monkey out of her yet," said Greg, following Ashley over the fence and leaving me to bring up the rear.

As I landed on the other side of the fence, heaping misery upon the flowerbed that had already been battered by three pairs of feet before me, I stood upright and took in my surroundings. Much more open than the neighbor's yard, this one—which I assumed backed up to Tom's childhood home—offered little or no cover. Not that cover would have done us much use, as the element of surprise had been massacred by Tom sprinting across the lawn, yelling, "Mom! Mom!"

"God, spare me from civilian intervention," I muttered. "What was Raphael thinking?"

"Looks like Mom's okay, though," said Greg, jerking his head toward the raised veranda where a middle-aged woman was rising to her feet in the shade, placing a glass of iced tea on the table beside her and holding her arms out to embrace Tom. As we came up behind mother and son, we could hear Tom saying the same thing over and over.

"Thank God you're safe, Mom, thank God you're safe."

"I'm safe," she replied, holding him at arms' length and gazing at him. "Good to see you, Tom, honey."

I didn't have long to ponder as Mrs. Morgan turned her gaze on us. "Who are your friends? Honey, why did you come over the fence? Why not just let yourself in at the front?"

"Um . . .you know, Pete and I always loved climbing those trees."

"Yes, honey, but it's a bit naughty to go trespassing in their garden when they're away."

A sudden idea popped into my head. "Who's away?" I asked abruptly. Mrs. Morgan released her son from her embrace and pushed him away, turning long-lashed blue eyes, startlingly like Tom's, in my direction.

"Why, the neighbors, of course," she said with a sweet smile.

"Mark and Susan Watson," replied Tom, looking at me with a puzzled frown. "I told you."

Darn! I wanted her to tell me. My gut was telling me something.

"Well, now you're here, can I get you anything? Iced tea? Soda?"

"No, no, we're just fine, thank you, Mrs. Morgan."

"Oh, call me, Lizzy, please."

"Since when do you go by Lizzy?" asked Tom.

Tom looked at his mom, a puzzled frown on his face, and my apprehension grew. Something wasn't right here, and I guessed Tom felt it too. I glanced at him, and our eyes met, mine sending a silent warning to him not to let on, his slight nod letting me know he'd understood.

Lizzy? Tom? Mrs. Morgan hates names being shortened.

"M-Mom, what happened?" asked Tom, stumbling slightly over the first word. I hoped Mrs. Morgan hadn't noticed, or if she had, I hoped she put it down to natural nervousness as a result of having heard his mom threatened at gunpoint earlier today when he was still a three-hour flight away. "I am so sorry I didn't warn you not to let Sanchez in."

"I don't think I'd have had much choice in the matter, honey," replied Mrs. Morgan. "He was quite persistent."

"So, where is he?"

"Oh, um . . .he got a call on his cell phone and took off."

"What, he just left?" asked Greg incredulously.

"Did he say where?" added Tom.

"No, honey, and I didn't want to get him to stay behind so that I could ask him."

"Understandable," said Greg. "I'm Gregory Livingstone, by the way," he added, holding a hand out to Mrs. Morgan, which she shook with something less than enthusiasm.

"Ashley Harrington," added Ashley, grabbing Tom's mom's hand before she had a chance to pull away and pumping it up and down. Before I could even hold my hand out, Mrs. Morgan started babbling.

"Hey, Tom, it's time to fetch the girls from their after-school ballet class. Do you want to go? They'll be so pleased to see you. They're at the same elementary school you went to."

"Of course, I can't wait to see them," said Tom, frowning. "Are you sure you're okay? I don't want to leave you alone."

"No, honey, you go. I'll be just fine."

"I could stay with you, Mrs. Morgan," I said as sweetly as I could. "My name's Kathryn. Kathryn Beck."

Mrs. Morgan's eyes darkened, and she shrank away from my outstretched hand as if it were a poisonous snake—which was ironic, since she was the one who hissed. It was barely audible, under her breath, but I heard it. And if I heard it, Ashley would have heard it.

It was then that I knew.

CHAPTER FIFTEEN

"I think we should all go fetch the girls. We've got a car parked just a short walk away," I said, standing right in Mrs. Morgan's face, crowding her personal space.

"It would be quicker to walk to the school," said Tom. "Come on, Mom, I'm sure a nice walk in the sunshine will do you good after your ordeal."

That hissing noise again. The game was up. Injecting a sugary sweetness into my voice, I put an end to the pretense.

"Perhaps you'd like to slip into something a little more comfortable first, Auntie Jacquelyn," I said, my eyes fixed on hers. "A pair of Jimmy Choo's, perhaps? Your own body, maybe? Whatever that looks like."

Without a word, Jacquelyn, still in the guise of Tom's mom, turned and disappeared into the house, slamming the door behind her. We heard the click-click of the bolts securing it from within before Tom took off around the side of the house.

"Give me strength!" I muttered, sprinting off in pursuit, the slap-slap-slap of footfalls telling me my teammates were right behind me. "Where's he going now?"

"Front," Ashley panted in my ear. "I guess he has a key. Hurry, before Jacquelyn bolts that too."

Skidding around the corner of the house, we saw the front door standing open. It looked like Tom had arrived first. Without hesitation, we followed him into the house and pulled up in a spacious hallway to get our bearings.

"Mom?" Tom's voice echoed around the open space as he took the wooden staircase in front of us two steps at a time. "Mom, where are you?"

"Is she here? Can you feel her?" I asked Ashley. The clairsentient member of the team was usually the one who could pick up on people's vibes before the rest of us. She looked around herself for a moment, then turned her attention to me.

"Who?" she asked. "Mrs. Morgan or Jacquelyn?"

I shuddered at the reminder of my connection to our arch-nemesis. "I meant Jacquelyn," I replied pointedly. "If you can feel Mrs. Morgan's presence, that would be cool."

Ashley looked around again. "Nope. No bad vibes."

"Did you get bad vibes out on the veranda?"

"Yeah, big time. When we arrived, I put it down to Sanchez having been here. Now, I know better. How about you?"

"Only when she called Tom 'Tom.' It jarred me. I guess I subconsciously remembered Tom telling us how Mrs. Morgan insists on him being called 'Thomas,' so I don't know if I can feel her presence."

"Well, I can," said Ashley. "Only I can't feel it anymore. So, I guess she's taken off."

Remembering the solitary raven flying away after the prison break a couple of days ago, I wondered at Ashley's choice of words.

"Guys!" Tom's shout from the second floor startled us all. "Up here."

As one, the three of us sprinted across the hall and up the stairs.

"Where, Tom?" called Greg.

"In here!"

We followed the sound of Tom's voice into a pleasant and airy bedroom, the array of perfumes and half-used makeup on the dresser telling us that this was Mrs. Morgan's room. Across the room from us, the door to a walk-in closet stood open, and the frantic murmurings from within told us that Tom was inside. Crossing the room, we crowded into the doorway and looked down to the floor, where he was cradling a woman, her head in his lap. She was unconscious—I hoped—her hair matted with dried blood, her hands and feet bound, the reddening of the skin and the deeper red of blood beneath the ropes that bound them telling us how roughly she had been treated. A discarded neckerchief lay at her side. I could only assume this filthy rag had been used to gag her.

"I left my cell phone in the car," he said, looking up at us. "Can one of you call 911?"

"No need," I said, stepping forward. "I got this."

Tom gave me a curious look, but he didn't argue. Instead, he said. "This is my mom, for sure. She smells right. That other woman didn't. She didn't feel right either. I knew. I knew as soon as she hugged me. Then she called me Tom, said her name was Lizzy. Mom's never anything other than Elizabeth. She likes to think she's the queen of England, you know?" Tom gave a sad laugh, which faded abruptly as he looked at me. "Kathryn, what are you doing?"

I held my arms outstretched before me. "Tom, you told me once you'd trust me with your life. You told me more recently, you meant it. Now you gotta trust me with your mom's life."

Tom looked down at Mrs. Morgan's battered face, glanced up at my outstretched arms. With only the slightest hesitation, he transferred his mom to my care. Supporting Mrs. Morgan's head with one arm, I put my other hand directly on her wound. It was hard to see underneath all the dried blood—why do head wounds always bleed so copiously? —but my hand instinctively knew where to rest.

Immediately, the familiar tingling shot up and down my arm, the warmth gathering. My skin and Mrs. Morgan's melded, my hand becoming part of her head as the heat overwhelmed us both. Purple light shot down my arm and into her wound, the gold specks enveloping both of us as the blood on her face dissolved into nothing, the gaping wound on her head knitting together and closing. Then the gold specks enveloped her whole body, and purple light shot to her wrists and ankles. The bindings dropped from her body without resistance, and the soreness and chafing beneath them paled and healed, leaving her skin smooth and undamaged. Only then did the specs fade, the purple light recede, the warmth chill.

Nothing to see here. Everything is normal.

Looking up at Tom, I expected to see the amazement on his face. Instead, he just smiled, full of warmth and gratitude and friendship.

"I know," he said. "I always knew you could do it. I just forgot for a moment."

"What do you mean you knew I could do it? How did you know?" I asked.

Before he was able to respond, I felt a movement in my arms. I looked at Mrs. Morgan again as her blue eyes, so like her son's, opened.

"Mom," Tom breathed.

"I'm okay, honey," she replied, sitting up. "I feel better than I have for a long time."

"You have Kathryn to thank for that."

Mrs. Morgan's eyes turned to meet mine. "Ah yes," she said, her next words took me completely by surprise. "David's girl. I guess he passed those good ole purple hands onto you."

"Uh . . . uh . . . I . . ."

With a laugh, Mrs. Morgan sat up and then got to her feet, turning to Greg and Ashley, who watched open-mouthed from the doorway.

"Thomas, you going to introduce your friends to me?"

Tom was as speechless as I was. He just stood and stared at his mom.

"Thomas? Response this year would be nice, honey. The girls' ballet class finishes soon."

"So, they are at class?" was all Tom could manage his voice crackling with concern.

"Yes, dear. Why?" she responded so calmly that it made me think she knew more than she was letting on.

"That's where you, well, she, said they were," Tom said.

"She?"

"Jacquelyn . . . she was pretending to be you, and we didn't notice until something didn't feel right, smell right. Just rest, Mother, it's a long story."

"Tom, aren't you worried about the children? If you knew it wasn't me, why didn't that set you into high gear to get them back with you?" Elizabeth said.

"Mother, why do I get the feeling you know more than you are letting on?" Tom leaned in closer, his face streaked with stress beads of sweat.

Collectively, our six pairs of eyes looked at each other. When my eyes met Ashley's, I saw panic—likely the same panic visible in my eyes. Jacquelyn had the girls. We had to leave. Now.

Tom jumped up, not letting me finish. "Let's go! Hurry!"

We rushed out of the house, following Tom downstairs through the kitchen, where he grabbed his keys from the counter, and out into the garage, unlocking the SUV with a chirp.

Mrs. Morgan continued talking as we piled into the car as if nothing was wrong. "I don't know why they didn't kill me, but Jacquelyn seemed to want me kept alive for some reason. I doubt it was affection for an 'old friend.'" Again, that pleasant laugh. I was beginning to like this brave woman. "I guess I was more useful as live bait."

We all piled into the SUV and Elizabeth talked as Tom navigated the SUV towards his kids' school, his mother's chatter keeping us distracted as we gazed outside at the lengthening shadows. It seemed that she expressed her nervousness through talking. Her joyful laugh made me smile despite the stressful situation.

"I was always Lizzy when we were kids. I hated it, but it stuck. That's all Jacquelyn ever knew me as. I wasn't about to correct her, or when she called you 'Tom,' Thomas. I knew, if you hadn't already worked it out, you'd know something was amiss when she used those wretched diminutives."

I laughed out loud. I couldn't help myself. "You'd get along well with Raphael."

Elizabeth Morgan turned a dazzling smile in my direction. "Oh, but I do, Kathryn, dear. Raphael and I go way back." Again, four mouths dropped open. Also, that musical giggle. "Was he with you when Sanchez and I had that little chat over the phone earlier?"

"He was," said Greg.

"We must have a catch-up sometime. Tell him he's a bad boy, not coming to visit me in all these years. Tell him he'll fall if he's not careful."

"Fall? Fall from where?"

"He'll know. So, Kathryn, to answer your earlier question 'How did you know?', well, your dad and I grew up together. Same road, same town, same school. I was quite sweet on him for a while. Lost touch when he met Jessica, but he did send a card when you were born. When I saw David's eyes looking down at me from your face, felt David's healing powers flowing through your hands, no introductions were necessary."

I stared at Elizabeth, in awe. She had grown up with Jacquelyn, my father, and Raphael.

"Have you noticed something?" whispered Ashley, sidling up beside me. "The shadows," said Ashley in a voice so low, I could barely catch the words. I'd heard enough, though. Ashley was entirely right. When we'd arrived at Elizabeth's place, the sun had been high in the sky; now, the shadows were lengthening as it set in the west. The school, a long, white one-story building with a gabled porchway above its entrance, was across the road from us, the sinking sun behind us casting dark stripes over its façade from the palm trees along the edge of the street. There wasn't a soul in sight.

"No!" cried Tom, running across the deserted road and up the school, the rest of us following. Even Elizabeth looked worried. "Where is everyone? Where are my kids?"

"This isn't right. There should be ballet and gymnastics going on inside, soccer practice on the field over there," said Elizabeth, leading us to follow her son around the side of the school building and pointing to an empty soccer field. "There should be cars lined up along the road, people waiting for their kids or watching the soccer game."

"Not at six thirty in the evening, I guess," said Ashley, looking at her watch.

"What? No, no, we pick the girls up from ballet at four thirty. I think soccer practice ends a bit later, but I'd guess everyone would be home by six thirty."

"Well, that's where everyone is then. Home." Ashley showed Elizabeth her watch, and the older woman's eyes widened in surprise.

Time had passed and we just didn't realize it. Somehow, we had lost three hours.

A roar of rage from the back of the school sent all of us sprinting in its direction. Skidding around the corner, I saw a furious Tom facing the school and hollering his lungs out. Opposite him, standing in a *V*-shape in front of a set of double doors, was a group of seven men, all looking like they were better endowed with muscles than brain cells. At the point of the *V*, smirking back at Tom, was the darkly handsome Sanchez. But it wasn't Sanchez and his goons who had upset Tom; his attention was fixed firmly on the large plate window to their left.

He was shrieking. "What in the name of all that's holy is . . . that?"

Elizabeth and I moved swiftly over to join him, with Greg and Ashley close behind us. Following his gaze, I was confronted by a sight the likes of which I had never seen before, and I sincerely hoped I would never see again.

The window opened onto what appeared to be a large room—possibly an assembly hall, or a dance studio—only it was difficult to make out any details thanks to the . . . the . . . thing that was occupying most of the space. Closing my eyes and opening them slowly, rubbing them with my knuckles—nothing made a difference.

The room was filled with what could only be described as a cloud—a living, breathing cloud. Dark and ominous, it shifted and pulsed, pressing against the window as if trying to escape, then curling back in on itself, twisting and turning, continually moving.

"That isn't anything holy, Tom," I murmured. No sooner had the words left my mouth than the cloud became agitated, billowing against the window and completely obliterating any view of the room.

A cloud. A school. Michael's premonition suddenly, horrifically, made sense.

A cloud. Like the one that took Dad.

"Do you see that?" asked Greg, appearing with Ashley at my side.

"Huh? Oh, yeah, I see it."

The air in front of us rippled, and then our focus changed. Instead of being outside looking in, we were inside the room, seeing three people huddled under a table. Two frightened girls—Emily and Rebecca Morgan, Tom's kids—were cowering on the floor, keeping themselves as low as possible while a man was doing his utmost to keep his body between them and wisps of darkness that kept flicking under the table like the forked tongues of snakes, attacking from all angles.

"Do you guys get that smell?" asked Tom, his voice unsteady, his gaze not wavering from the horror inside the school.

"No."

"Yes," said Ashley. "Kind of odd, a bit like smoke from a bonfire." It seemed hearing and empathy weren't Ashley's only heightened senses.

"That's the same smell I got back at the house. You know, when I hugged my mom, who wasn't my mom."

"You mean that thing inside the schoolroom is . . . is . . ." I said.

I hadn't realized Sanchez had walked over to stand right in front of us until he spoke, making us all cringe. "Jacquelyn has been expecting you."

CHAPTER SIXTEEN

"My kids!" said Tom, turning to glare at Sanchez. "Where are my kids?"

Sanchez laughed. It was the antithesis of Elizabeth's joyful giggle—a sound so devoid of pleasure and happiness, and it was chilling to hear.

"Oh, they're just fine. Jacquelyn's looking after them."

"You mean they're in there?" His expression was horrified, his eyes never leaving Sanchez's face. Tom pointed toward the schoolroom. All the time, the abomination inside the school continued to swirl and writhe.

"It's okay, Michael's in there with them," I said. I guessed Sanchez would already be aware of Michael's presence, and it seemed more appropriate at that moment to lower Tom's stress levels as much as possible than keep Michael's intervention a secret.

"For all the good it'll do any of them, yes, your friend is in there too. He tried to reason with us. Ask us to take him instead of the girls." Sanchez's grin revealed straight white teeth in a tanned, strong-jawed face. He should have been gorgeous. He wasn't. "Children work so much better as bargaining chips than adults, don't you think?"

"My daughters are not bargaining chips!" spat Tom. "What sort of man are you to allow kids to be caught up in your boss's twisted game?"

"An ambitious man," replied Sanchez, the cold smile still in place. "A man who recognizes an opportunity when it arises. I like to think of myself as a pragmatic man."

"Yeah? I like to think of you as an evil creep."

I butted in before Tom lost it entirely and did something we'd all regret. Already, Sanchez's muscular goons formed a human wall behind him, their muscles rippling, scowling at Tom.

"You mentioned bargaining, Sanchez," I said, shouldering Tom out of the way so I was face-to-face with Jacquelyn's latest right-hand man. "So, what's the bargain?"

"Ah, you're ready to talk, huh?" Sanchez looked me square in the eye. "The deal on the table is simple. The Morgan girls in exchange for you, Kathryn Bek."

"And Michael?"

"He made his own choice. Jacquelyn may let him go; she may not. That decision is hers alone. Just the girls. That's all I can guarantee."

I was silent, glancing around at my team—at Elizabeth, whose eyes were glassy; at Tom, whose face was pinched with worry. Greg was staring at the school, his forehead creased in concentration; Ashley glanced from him to Elizabeth, her eyes widening in surprise as they met those of the older woman. All this I took in during the few seconds it took for Sanchez's patience to run out.

"So, what's it going to be, Bek? Save your sorry skin, or save those poor, frightened, innocent little girls." The mock concern in Sanchez's voice made my blood boil, and I could see Tom's body tense in anger. Before he could react, I gave the only answer I could, Raphael's voice from long ago echoing in my ears.

"So long as you do what feels right with what you see, things will often work out better than human averages dictate."

"Take me. Free the girls."

"Excellent," drawled Sanchez. I looked around, almost expecting to see Mr. Burns from *The Simpsons* standing beside me. Instead, I saw three of the muscle-bound goons manhandling an odd contraption toward me.

Where has that come from?

It could be best described as a large test tube, large enough for an adult human, with a low plinth covering the end that would generally be open. The test tube was carried slowly over to us, then the goons stood it upright on its plinth, a doorway opening from nowhere, appearing out of the solid glass of its side.

"In you go," said Sanchez. "We can't have you playing that silly laying-on-of-hands trick on Jacquelyn again, now, can we?"

"I got a real bad feeling about this, Kate," warned Greg.

To my surprise and slight dismay, Ashley contradicted him. "Do as Sanchez says, Kate," she advised.

"For my girls' sake," added Tom.

That did it. What sort of team leader would I be if I allowed two kids to suffer because I had no backbone? I stepped into the test tube, the doorway closed immediately behind me, and the glass walls were stable again. Strangely, the air was fresh inside. I could see, hear, even smell everything going on around me; I just couldn't touch or influence it in any way. I felt the smooth glass wall surrounding me. There was no way I'd be laying hands on anyone through that.

It was down to the team to resolve this one without their leader.

Ashley was speaking to Sanchez. "So, you got Kate. What now?"

"Yeah, my kids?" said Tom. "Your side of the bargain."

Sanchez laughed again, that hard, humorless sound that made me shudder. "Did I say we'd struck a bargain? Careless of me. Or, careless of you to believe me. Jacquelyn's had a tough time recently." Laugh. Shudder. "You wouldn't deny her a bit of fun, would you?"

"No!" screamed Tom, lunging at Sanchez. The goons piled forward as one. It was all I could do to keep my eyes on them; this didn't look like it would end well.

I should have known better. I should have trusted in the process. One day I'd learn.

Then I watched as Elizabeth whispered to Tom, watched Sanchez frown as Tom smiled. "Now, Thomas!" Elizabeth commanded.

Tom raised his hands, palms facing toward the school, and a jet of blinding white light shot from them, shattering the plate glass window and rocketing straight into the rippling, angry cloud that was pouring from the large gap where the window used to be. The streams of light collided at speed with the cloud, setting off sparks from within like some sort of freaky electrical storm.

The cloud imploded.

It folded in on itself before bursting into a million pieces, flying outward in all directions. Tom, Ashley, Greg, and Elizabeth threw themselves to the ground. Sanchez turned tail and ran. *Some right-hand man he is*, I thought. I could do nothing but stand trapped in my test tube as fragments of darkness battered the outside of it.

As I turned to follow the fragments' trajectory, I saw them starting to gather once again. From all around, dark blobs congregated over by the school gate, knitting together to take on the form of a tall, slim woman in a business suit and impossibly high Jimmy Choo's.

Jacquelyn was here.

Her army of men surrounded us.

Wait. I thought, *Jacquelyn was here.* I could have sworn that was her, but as I squinted to see more clearly, I saw the scene of hostages, goons surrounding everyone, and . . . Dad?

"Dad?" I yelled out. I hadn't seen this man since I was five. He was only a memory, yet it was him. I heard his voice. I could sense his presence.

"Cinnamon? Where are you, Cinnamon?" the voice came back.

My heart began to beat faster, and I thought to myself: How is this even remotely possible?

"Dad, you say?" and without a flinch, Jacquelyn's voice pierced through my eardrums. "Daddy looking for his little Cinnamon—how excruciatingly sweet."

A cyclone of gray dust—and my dad was gone, and she was there. This was going to be a knockdown drag-out. I could just feel it.

Where did my dad go? Was that just a vision?

Jacquelyn just materialized. There are hostages inside. I am trapped, and that aunt of mine has her goons surrounding everyone.

I immediately realized that nothing around me was real. It was as if I was a hologram—my spirit was alive, but my body itself was purely a three-dimensional rendering. So, I sat with that idea for a moment, and I closed my eyes. *If I am a hologram, then I am not really inside this tube, am I? I am not being held "captive," and I can make my own choices because that is what free will is all about.*

The ground trembled beneath me, a purple haze spun from the top of my head, expanding to engulf my entire body, and—as if by magic, or some inconceivable wrinkle in the rules of physics—I shifted right out of the tube and onto the ground.

I didn't have time to think, to react, or to consider any of what just happened, but I knew it was real.

I took a step toward Jacquelyn, my fist clenched at my side. I was ready to end this once and for all. Her eyes widened in terror. "How . . . how are you doing that?"

An SUV sped onto the school grounds, driving on the asphalt path that winds around the playground. It stopped right beside Jacquelyn. She opened the back door, climbed inside, and the driver stepped on the gas, spun the car around with a screech, and roared out of sight.

I listened to the sound of the engine fading away down the quiet road outside the school gates for a few moments, then turned to look back toward the others. Tom was gazing at his hands in wonder as if seeing them for the first time, and Elizabeth was beaming her approval at everyone.

And then came the words that made my heart skip a beat, and my mind question reality.

"Daddy! Daddy!"

Two figures in leotards and dance tights leaped over the sill of the glassless window and sprinted toward Tom, flinging themselves into his arms as he hugged them tightly, tears streaming down his face. He kissed their hair and repeated their names over and over. Elizabeth swooped toward them and wrapped her arms around her son and granddaughters, her face shining with joy and relief. Ashley's hand stole into one of Greg's, holding on to it tightly as he finally raised his eyes to meet hers and smiled sheepishly.

Michael then climbed over the low windowsill and strolled across to his teammates. He clapped a hand on each of their shoulders and broke into a tuneless rendition of the old John Paul Young song, "Love is in the Air." They all laughed. I laughed too.

Smiling so widely my face was starting to ache, I threw my arms around my team, doing my best to envelop them all at once.

"Uh-oh," said Greg.

"Public display of affection alert," added Michael.

"Emergency! Emergency! HGS team leader loses the plot in unprecedented emotional meltdown."

"Yeah, yeah, you know you love me, really," I said, beaming indulgently at my team. My family. "Do you know what I want more than anything right now? Grilled cheese sandwich, up on the roof of the brownstone."

"Hot dogs," added Greg.

"Beer!" That from Michael, naturally.

"Home," Ashley concluded, the wistfulness in her voice resonating with all of us.

I looked over at the Morgan family group. "Home," I repeated. "It looks like our work here is done."

"Do you think they'll remember any of it?" asked Greg.

Elizabeth raised her eyes, looked right at us, and nodded. "Tom maybe. The girls? I think not. I hope not."

Emily and Rebecca were talking excitedly, arms waving as they related the highlights of their day. As we watched, they turned and caught sight of me and let out whoops of delight.

"Kathryn! Kathryn!" cried Emily as she and her younger sister raced over to greet me with the unbridled joy of the young. "We haven't seen you in, like, ages! What are you doing in Miami?"

"Oh," I replied airily, "we were here on business. These are the people I work with." I gestured at Ashley, Greg, and Michael, and Emily uttered a heartfelt, "Cool." Yeah, I guess we are pretty cool.

I was weak, but the girls were so happy at being reunited with their father to notice or care.

"Daddy's been away for, like, ages. Mommy too. I hope she comes home soon."

"So do I, honey," I said with feeling, ruffling Rebecca's hair. Jessica was a good mom for all her faults, and these sweet girls deserved to have her back in their lives. Sadly, my instinct told me that this particular story wasn't destined to have a happy ending.

Luckily, the girls had bounced on to a new idea. "Kathryn, are you going to stay for a few days? Say you will!"

"Oh, please! Please!"

"Girls, I think Kathryn has had a busy day," said Elizabeth, coming over to join us. "I'm guessing she and her friends just want to get home. I'm sure we'll all meet one day again."

"Yes," I said, meeting Elizabeth's gaze and smiling warmly at her. "I'm sure of it too."

CHAPTER SEVENTEEN

My gosh, were we glad to get back to Manhattan and all that was familiar to us. It was late when we finally piled out of the taxi that Raphael had sent us up from the airfield and into the brownstone. None of us spoke as we headed for the stairs.

We debriefed on Wednesday morning, with Raphael having taken pity on us and given us Tuesday to recover our strength. He told us that Ms. Jerilyn had been ready and eager to share all she knew in return for a new identity and a chance to start over again. I wasn't sure how successful a woman who was so ready to betray her former allies would be at building a decent life for herself. Still, as Raphael said, she was too terrified of the possible repercussions—from both the HGS and Jacquelyn—to consider doing anything but behaving impeccably from now on. Ms. Clare and the others who had been recruiting on Jacquelyn's behalf had been rounded up and arrested—I was a little shocked at how many of the guards had been corrupted but was relieved not to see Ms. Washington's name on the list. I suppose I had known Ms. Washington's name wouldn't appear— there was nothing remotely evil about that woman. I'd genuinely liked Ms. Washington and was happy to know that my instincts had served me well regarding her excellent character too. The two Alaskan prisons had been closed, and the falsely accused were released, with promises that their records would be sealed. I was delighted to learn that both Christina and Krystal lived nearby—Christina in Queens and Krystal in the Hamptons.

Once Raphael was done, I took the stand and summarized our time in Florida. Glancing at Raphael as I outlined Tom's contribution to our latest defeat of Jacquelyn, I had expected to see at least a flicker of surprise. Instead, he just smiled benignly back at me and murmured, "Good, good."

"Oh, and Elizabeth Morgan says you need to go visit her," I said, somewhat aggressively. As usual, Raphael wasn't fazed by my tone.

"Ah, as usual, the lovely Elizabeth is quite right!" he said cheerfully. "Remiss of me, and something I will rectify without further ado." He made for the door, leaving me standing at the head of the conference room.

"So, is that it?" I asked Raphael's retreating form. "Meeting over?"

Raphael turned and looked at me. "Oh, I do beg your pardon, Kathryn. How rude of me. I'm just so excited to see Elizabeth again. Yes, I think the debrief is complete, so why don't you take a few weeks off? Get some R & R, recharge your batteries, that kind of thing. Heaven knows"—and when Raphael says, "heaven knows," you believe him— "you guys have earned it. Reconvene in mid-October." Raphael made for the door again, then something struck him, and he turned to look directly at me. "By the way, Kathryn, what did you make of Elizabeth Morgan?"

"I liked her," I replied simply.

"Just liked?"

I looked at Raphael in confusion. What more did he want me to say?

"Well, um . . . I kind of felt I could trust her. Instinctively, you know. You know sometimes you meet someone, and you feel like you've known them your whole life. It was a little bit like that."

Raphael nodded. "Well, that's hardly surprising." Then, he walked from the room, leaving me to wonder what he meant.

"C'mon, Team Leader Bek," said Michael. "You heard Raphael. Staycation starts here, and I vote we waste no more time at work. How's about we start with that grill and beers up on the roof, like we were just talking about on Monday?"

"You got it, Team Member Odin," I replied, taking his outstretched hand, and stepping down from the presentation platform. "You're on beers. Greg, you can get the veggie burgers and hot dogs, I'll take salads and cheese grills—naturally—and Ashley, you can bring along something sweet for dessert. Deal?"

"Deal!"

It always amazes me just how fast time flies by when you're having a good time. We sure did have a good time over the free weeks that Raphael had given us, taking a few days in the Hamptons, so Ashley and I could reconnect with Krystal, and spending a raucous afternoon with Christina at her place in Queens, cooking out in her backyard and chugging beer—if she was a good cook with limited supplies in prison, she blew me away with what she could create from fresh ingredients. We chilled in Central Park and shopped till we dropped—the guys too. I was the only one on the team who wasn't a dedicated follower of fashion, but I couldn't help getting carried away by their enthusiasm. I felt a thrill as I hung all my new clothes up in my closet. Scott managed to join us each weekend, and I savored every single quality moment I spent with him. After my ordeal in Alaska, I would never take his love and companionship—or my freedom—for granted again, and of course, we made the most of the pleasant late-summer weather and ate on the roof of the brownstone most every evening.

"Dinner up top," Ashley announced, a gleam of excitement in her eyes as she joined me in the living room the weekend before we were due to reconvene in the HGS offices at nine a.m. Monday.

"Just by way of a change," I said, laughing. "Yeah, sounds great to me. Do you want me to pick up some stuff or make salads or anything?"

"No, you just leave it to Greg and me, we will take care of everything."

"Oh, okay. Well, gosh, that is nice of you. Can I give you some money or something?" I suggested, reaching for my wallet.

"No, Kate, let's not worry about all of that. I'll tell you what you can be in charge of—the ginger ale and cherries, okay?"

"Perfect." I loved ginger ale with a cherry. It was my go-to drink if I felt like being fancy without the buzz of champagne, and I thought it was just as pretty when poured into a cut-glass goblet.

"Hey, Kate, can I talk to you about something?"

"Sure—shoot."

Ashley plopped down on the couch and crossed her legs.

"Since we've been off work, I've been participating in daily meditation, and it's helping. The person hosting it has different call-in times, mornings and evenings, and the vibrations—he calls them frequencies—that he works within enormously help clear things up. At least, I've found it helpful for me on a variety of levels, and not just to get rid of old thoughts or dreams or whatever."

She paused.

"I think we've got to be prepared that we're going to have to face something major in the future, something worse than anything we've faced yet. Remember what Jacquelyn's henchman Turner said before he died, that nothing can stop the horror Jacquelyn and her followers have already launched on the world? We've got to be prepared; we've got to stop it. Anyway, the meditation practice helps me . . . not make sense of the dreams as such but treat them as possible warnings. Keep them in mind rather than getting so freaked out by them. We never know when they might be useful, so I'm learning to store them in my long-term memory, to access them when I need them."

I nodded, listening.

"I always felt like I was safe, protected, and now I feel like there is no safe place, and at any minute, life could change."

"I get it."

"So, that's why . . . well . . ." Then she blurted out the words I never expected to hear from her. "That's why when we have the barbeque on the roof, I want you to be my maid of honor because I am marrying Greg."

"What?" I could only imagine that I looked white as a ghost as I felt every drop of blood drain out of my face.

"We've been together for a while, but we've been keeping it quiet. I don't want Michael and Scott to know. This is going to be one of those . . . well, you know, surprise events."

"You . . . and Greg . . . getting married . . . well, this is great, Ashley, really great! I apologize for looking so shocked, but you have to give me that—I had no idea things had gotten so serious between you guys."

"I just wanted to tell you and ask if you would do this for me."

"Absolutely."

And just like that, everything changed—again.

CHAPTER EIGHTEEN

"Hey, team, conference room," Raphael yelled down the hall.

We all got up from our desks and headed toward the Fishbowl, the name we had given to the conference room since it is surrounded in glass. Anybody passing by can see in and watch what's going on, and they often do. Raphael watched from the presentation stand as we filed in and sat down, then without preamble, he took Michael and me entirely by surprise.

"I have an announcement. Next year, Ashley will be leaving the team."

The room fell quiet. Michael and I turned to face Ashley, our mouths open. Greg simply looked sheepish, and Ashley gave us a broad smile.

"There's nothing wrong," she said. "It's just that . . . well, I won't be able to continue fieldwork once the baby comes."

"Baby?" Michael yelled and ran over to Ashley, nearly knocking her off her chair as he grabbed her in a bear hug and squeezed her.

"Yes, baby," Raphael confirmed. "So, I have told her that she could become our administrator and work with Barry here at headquarters."

"So, are we going to be a team of three out in the field?" I asked. "We work better as four. Complement each other, you know?"

"Agreed—four is the ideal."

"So, who's joining us? Scott?"

"Scott has his line of work. For now, though, Ashley says she is fine to carry on with the rest of you on missions, so it's not urgent we find a replacement straight away."

"So, Ashley, when are you due?" Michael asked.

"About six months," said Ashley, blushing. "Y'know, when we got out of the prison mission, Greg and I didn't waste any more time pretending we didn't have feelings for each other."

"Well, congratulations—to both of you."

Greg was still just sitting there, looking at Ashley and kind of spacing out.

"You okay, Greg?" I leaned over closer to him.

"I am ecstatic. I'm so happy and excited . . . and scared. How am I going to cope with being a dad?"

Everybody in the room laughed.

"Talking of missions," said Raphael authoritatively, and we all calmed down and turned our attention back to him, "Kathryn, I need you and the team to head to Chicago. You are scheduled for a meeting in Hyde Park on Tuesday with a few of the city aldermen. There are rumblings from the Twenty-Fourth Street Mafia, and we need to intervene."

"Um, any chance of a few more details?" asked Greg.

"For the longest time, this section of the mafia has been protected, I'm not sure by whom or how they do it, but they always seem to walk away from any and all situations without a scratch on them. This time it went too far. There was an explosion at Comiskey Park. In reviewing the crime scene, among the debris remained a dozen gold bars and multiple dead bodies. We need to dig in and uncover what happened, who was involved, and why Comiskey Park.

"That's all I can really say for now. Oh, except—perhaps while you are there, you can have some pizza as a team, it's really terrific. A nice jog by the lakefront is always pleasurable." Raphael said with an impish grin.

"No, Raphael, I mean mission-critical details," Greg said.

"Oh, that . . . well, it's the usual," said Raphael. "Keep your eyes open, trust your instincts, work with what you see."

"Gee, thanks," I said. "Clear as mud, as usual, Raphael."

He just turned and grinned at us, collected his things, and left the room.

"Okay, team," I ordered, "let's get on it."

The meeting adjourned, we rose and started heading for the door.

"Hold on a minute, Kate. I need to speak with you privately," Raphael said.

What now? I thought. I didn't know if I could take any more surprises.

My teammates eyed me curiously, wondering what Raphael had up his sleeve. His expression was, as always, inscrutable, so I didn't know if this was good or bad. Was I going to be commended? Reprimanded? Had I made some grievous error? Was he going to demote me from my leadership role?

When the others were gone, a heavy silence settled over the room.

"Sit down." He sighed. "What I'm about to tell you is perhaps beyond your comprehension. But you've been at HGS long enough to know that nothing is beyond the realm of possibility. To always, if you'll pardon the cliché, expect the unexpected."

"You can say that again," I said.

"Do you believe in angels, Kate?"

In truth, my feelings about God, angels, demons, heaven and hell, and all that stuff were complicated, and I was still working out what I really believed.

"Basically, yes. I think so," I said.

"Well, they are real. And you walk among them."

I didn't know what to say or even what that meant.

"The angels have been lurking in the shadows for centuries. And you and your teammates are descended from them. That is why you were chosen. Michael is from the line of Gabriel; Ashley, the line of Uriel; Greg, the line of Chamuel and you, Kate, you are from the lineage of Michael."

My mouth opened but not a word came out. I was stunned. Finally, I stammered, "This, but . . . how could this be?"

"All the answers will be revealed to you in time," he said cryptically. "But I'm telling you this now because you are the leader of this team, and you deserve to know the full extent of the battle we are facing. Our struggle is bigger than criminals against the law-abiding, bigger than a secret agency fighting a shadowy criminal network that covets global domination, bigger even than 'good vs. evil.' Our fight is a celestial one; it transcends Earth itself. What we are facing—what you all will have to face from now on—is nothing less than the ageless battle between the warriors of heaven and the demons of hell. And by virtue of your lineage, you have been chosen to take up the sword and shield and lead this fight."

He paused. "If not, humanity itself will perish."

Raphael gazed into my eyes, a gaze full of gentle warmth and strength, but also something I had never really seen before—fear. The fate of the world hung on his shoulders. And now, too, on mine.

"I have about a million questions!" I blurted out.

He laughed. "I know. Like, I said—in time, you will understand. For now, go in peace, be with your team, with your husband, and rest. Today, we celebrate. Tomorrow, well—we will see what tomorrow brings."

ACKNOWLEDGMENTS

W hat do these words have in common?

Facetious	Exquisite	Thankful	Calliope
Loving	Henceforth	Kerfuffle	Joyful

Each of these words is a word that is not used enough.
Think about it - when was the last time you said CALLIOPE in a sentence?

For those who were part of the "book two team", each of you are brave, smart, courageous, supportive, kind . . . and I am honored, thankful and joyful that you are on this journey with me!

A special thank you and acknowledgement to Phyllis Green. I have never met Ms. Green, but she wrote one of my favorite books (and the first book I ever purchased at a Scholastic Book Fair) entitled *Nantucket Summer*. THANK YOU for writing that book! The impact of your work continues to bring joy to my life.

A NOTE TO YOU, THE READER

Thank you. You are the best!!! I could not have imagined a more dynamic supportive group of readers – please continue to leave reviews, and continue to buy the book, gift the book, and showcase the book with family, friends, and on social media.

I leave you with something that fellow Author Iain S. Thomas says – and it fits each of you perfectly:

"I need you to understand something. I wrote this for you. I wrote this for you and only you. Everyone else who reads it, doesn't get it. They may think they get it, but they don't. This is the sign you've been looking for. You were meant to read these words."

Until book three ...

You're 2 Good
+ 2 Be
4 Gotten

ABOUT THE AUTHOR

McKinley Aspen is a writer who lives in the Southern United States. In addition to the normal family shenanigans, McKinley has a busy schedule as "Chief Dog Walker" to Otis the puppy dog.

A graduate of both University of Chicago and Elmhurst University, McKinley enjoys exporing the world through family road trips, meals featuring Portillo's Beef with mozz (that's mozzarella in case you didn't know), and St. Louis Cardinals baseball.

If you haven't joined the mailing list, please jump over to the website https://McKinleyAspen.com or click on the QR code on the back cover and add your name. Sign up for free swag and news of upcoming book releases, signings, and appearances.

Made in United States
North Haven, CT
20 August 2023

40529250R00093